Teacher's Pet: A Dark Professor Romance

Penelope Ryan

A couple nights of pure bliss, letting my hot biology professor lay his hands on my body and have his way with me—all to save my failing grade and my future?
The choice seemed simple.
But everything is far from simple now.

Violet Sloan is failing biology. Which wouldn't be that big of a problem if she didn't need this class in order to graduate in three months. But she does. And on the other side of it is a bright future: her dream job already lined up, an incredible salary, and a career she can't wait to start. She just needs to pass this class. It doesn't help that her biology professor is hot as hell and just a tad bit distracting.

When Violet gets a failing grade on her latest exam, she meets with Professor Henry in an act of desperation. There, she realizes her professor might be just as distracted by her. After a few flirtatious encounters, he offers her some extra credit—a deal to save her grade. A deliciously dangerous deal she can't help but take him up on.

Only Violet has a track record of falling for the guys she sleeps with. And they have a track record of leaving. And as her arrangement with Professor Henry spirals out of control, she wonders whether she was truly ready to take this plunge.

A steamy erotic romance, this book is as hot as they come. Contains themes of rough play, BDSM, dirty talk, dominance, and humiliation.
Please note: this book contains taboo themes and relationships.

Chapter 1

Holy shit, he's hot.

I sigh, propping my elbows up on my desk, my chin in my palms. I gaze up at the front of the classroom, past the rows of desks in front of me, to Professor Alex Henry, his back to the class as he scrawls something on the board in chalk. His tailored suit fits him perfectly. Almost too perfectly. How are there even mass-made suits that fit a perfect body like that? My gaze wanders to his ass. God.

"Homework for this assignment is due next week, and I expect a bit more effort this time," he says, shooting the whole class a meaningful look. His eyebrows knit together in disgruntlement—but it only makes him hotter.

Jesus.

Who thought my senior year of college I'd be drooling over one of my professors? In what world does this happen? It's almost embarrassing. But honestly, anyone who looks at him would end up thinking the same deliciously dirty thoughts I am.

It doesn't hurt that he's nothing like the other professors. Not old and musty, not crabby. Well, maybe a little crabby. But definitely not old or musty. I'd peg him at twenty-eight or so. Maybe older, maybe younger. It's hard to say. He's definitely young for a professor.

What matters is that Biology 101 is a breath of fresh air compared to my other classes. It's a shame I hadn't needed any classes from him earlier. My major is English, and since I need a science credit to meet my basics, here I am.

I sigh in disappointment at the thought. Lucky biology majors.

The only problem is that Professor Henry's hotness is the only good thing about this class. Because I suck at science. Anything not directly English-related, and I'm honestly awful at it. This entire semester has been an absolute drag, and I've been hanging on by a thread.

In fact, I'm slightly worried I might not make it through this class. It's a panicked thought I've been pushing away all semester, but as the weeks continue and my grade doesn't improve, I'm starting to get more and more nervous. I need to pass this class in order to graduate in May—just a few months from now—and so far, that seems … difficult.

I'm considering tutoring for the first time in my life. I groan internally at the thought.

"Okay, looks like we're good for today," Professor Henry says, glancing at the clock. "See you all next class." He wipes his hands on his dress pants, leaving a slight smudge of chalk.

With one last glance at his wavy, dark hair, I gather up my things and follow the line of students out the door.

I glance down at my phone as I head out into the hallway. A text from Kayla waits on my screen. She's already waiting for me in the campus cafeteria where we typically grab lunch most days.

Kayla and I were paired as roommates freshman year and had immediately hit it off, continuing to room together every year of college. Currently, we share an apartment off campus together. Like me, she's an English major, although her goal is to continue on with her Master's and PhD and become a professor.

My goals fall a bit more into the private sphere. Publishing. In fact, I already have a job lined up after I graduate. I can barely believe it, but it's true. I was lucky enough to intern for a local publishing house here in Seattle my sophomore year. They'd loved me and invited me back junior year, and at the end of that internship I'd been offered a full-time editorial assistant position once I graduate.

I'd spent the entire week after that pinching myself and thanking my lucky stars. It's exactly the kind of job I'd dreamed of.

All the more reason to pass this damn biology class and actually graduate.

Fuck. One more thing to add to my to-do list.

I make my way across campus. Kensington University isn't a huge school, and its campus is very walkable. It only takes me about twenty minutes to meet Kayla at the main cafeteria where she's already waiting for me with one of her signature salads. I grab a sandwich and take a seat across from her at the table.

She grins up at me. "So, I got us some wine and everything we could possibly need for the perfect charcuterie board for tonight," she declares.

I laugh. Tonight's the premiere of the newest *Bachelor* series, and we're both avid fans. Avid fans of any reality TV show, really. It's great, after a long day or night of studying, to sit down and veg out in front of the TV while watching some silly reality show. It's our favorite pastime. "Perfect," I say.

"I have high hopes for this guy," Kayla continues. "He seems like a good catch."

"And the drama is going to be unparalleled," I add.

She rolls her eyes. "Always."

I bite into my sandwich and munch away.

"How was class?" Kayla asks. "The one with the hot professor, right?" She raises her eyebrows.

I roll my eyes, stifling a laugh. Then I sigh, dropping my sandwich to my plate. "Fine. I'm starting to get worried."

Kayla frowns. "Your grade's still not getting better?"

I shake my head, grimacing.

"I've never known you to get anything lower than an A minus," she mutters.

I throw my hands up in the air. "I know! That's why this is so infuriating."

"C's get degrees," she reminds me with a shrug.

"That's the thing though, I'm starting to worry I won't even get by with a C," I admit, nerves dancing in my belly at just the thought.

She widens her eyes. "Really?"

I nod, slightly embarrassed, but mostly just desperate.

She purses her lips. "Have you met with your professor?"

I pause. The idea hadn't occurred to me, actually. "I was thinking maybe I'd try to find someone to tutor me."

She nods. "Yeah. But I'd meet with your professor first. Maybe he has some tips or ideas or something?"

"That's a good idea," I admit. Honestly, the idea of meeting with him is just … nerve wracking. All I'd be able to think about is how hot he is. And how embarrassed I am to have such a terrible grade. We've never really spoken one-on-one, but he obviously knows I'm basically failing his class. It's not like it's a secret. I sigh in defeat. "Yeah, I'll reach out to him."

Kayla smiles. "But for tonight, all we need to think about is *Bachelor*." She wiggles her fingers in the air, and I laugh.

Chapter 2

I stand in the hallway of Oliver Hall, outside Professor Henry's office. The hallway is lined with offices for professors in the humanities, as well as a few classrooms. I'd emailed him last night about my predicament—my worry about failing his class—and he'd suggested I come see him today during office hours.

I straighten my shirt and run my fingers through my hair, suddenly overwhelmingly self-conscious. I almost immediately roll my eyes at myself.

You're his student, Violet, I snap at myself. *It doesn't matter what you look like.*

That doesn't stop me from flipping my hair a few times before gingerly knocking on the door.

"Come in," a deep voice calls out.

I open the door and tentatively step into the office. It's darker in here, with only a desk lamp giving off a warm glow. There are bookshelves lining the walls, and a dark mahogany desk behind which Professor Henry sits.

His dark wavy hair, short enough to be professional but long enough to appear tousled, looks so soft I could run my fingers through it.

Fuck. *Shut up, Violet.*

He smiles. "Come in, Violet."

I do as he says, closing the door behind me.

He gestures to the chair across from his desk, and I sit.

"So," he starts. "Tell me what's going on." He leans forward, resting his elbows on the desk.

Nerves dance in my belly. I take a deep breath. "Well," I start. "I'm not doing very well in your class." I give a nervous chuckle. "As I'm sure you know."

"You mean you don't love my class?" he asks with a smirk.

My face reddens. "I ..."

He chuckles, leaning forward and resting a hand on mine across the desk. The gesture is innocent, normal, but it sends a spark of electricity through my body. "I'm kidding," he says. "I know it's not everyone's cup of tea." He laughs again, leaning back in his chair.

I smile, relaxing slightly. "I ... don't know what to do," I admit. "I've been trying. I've been studying, going over the material. But I just keep ... doing terribly."

Professor Henry nods again, thinking. "What's your major?" he asks.

"English."

"Ah. Very different."

I smile and nod. "Exactly. And I normally do very well," I go on. "I know it's probably hard for you to believe, but before your class, I'd never gotten below an A minus in my life."

His eyes sparkle. "Oh, I'm dealing with a genius, am I?"

I can feel myself flushing again.

He stares me down, aware of my embarrassment and seemingly enjoying it. There's a twinkle in his eye that feels playful. Almost … flirtatious?

I almost physically shake my head. *No, Violet. You are projecting your ridiculous fantasies on to real life. There's no way your hot professor is actually flirting with you.*

"Well, Violet the Genius," he says, his amused smirk growing, "I can see how that would be frustrating."

I nod.

"I do have supplemental materials online," he suggests. "Flashcards I've created and the like. Have you looked into those?"

I shake my head. "No, I'd just studied my own notes."

"Try those. Everything on those flashcards and note sheets online correspond directly with my exams and assignments."

"Okay," I agree. "I'll definitely look at those."

"And there's tutoring through the biology department. The biology majors get paid for it through the school, so they're always more than willing."

"Yeah, I was considering that."

"Start with those things and let me know if you're still struggling," he says.

I smile. "Thanks, I will." I stand, grabbing my backpack and slinging it over my shoulder. "Thanks for meeting with me."

He smiles, the glint in his eyes sending a wave of nervous excitement through me. "It was nice chatting with you, Violet."

I leave his office and make my way down the hall, my footsteps echoing across the linoleum. His last word echoes through my mind. The way he'd said my name. The prettiest it's ever sounded. *Violet.*

Chapter 3

"This car is going to be the death of me, I swear," I say into the phone, staring in exasperation at my 2000 Dodge Durango in the campus parking lot.

"Do you want me to call a tow truck?" Kayla asks on the other end of the line. "I can come pick you up in the meantime."

I sigh, thinking of the many towing bills I've had to pay over the years for this car. I glance around. It's late, almost dusk. There are barely any other cars in the parking lot. I'd stayed late studying with a tutor in the biology building. I'd connected with him last week after my meeting with Professor Henry and have met with him a handful of times since then. The good news is I think I'm starting to actually get the hang of things. I'm less worried about failing the class.

The bad news is now I'm stranded on campus with a dead car.

"It's fine," I tell her. "I'll call a tow service. I will probably need a ride though. Let me figure out how long this'll take, and I'll call you back."

Kayla wishes me luck, and we hang up.

Hands on my hips, I glare daggers at my car.

"Need help?" a voice calls, momentarily startling me. I spin around to see a man exiting the biology building, and it takes me a few seconds to realize who it is.

Professor Henry.

Butterflies flutter in my stomach. "Oh. Hi," I call awkwardly.

He approaches, glancing at my car. "I saw you on the phone as I was leaving," he says—somewhat awkwardly as well. "You seem distressed. Everything okay?"

"Oh yeah, everything's fine," I assure him. "It's just my car won't start. It does that sometimes." I glance at it.

Concern washes over his face. "Oh."

"It's fine though," I tell him. "I'll just call a tow. I do it a lot." I offer a self-deprecating laugh.

"Why don't we try and jump it first?" Professor Henry offers. "I have cables in my car." He gestures to it across the parking lot.

I shake my head. It's embarrassing enough to have him find my like this, and I don't want to bother him and eat into his night. He's here late enough already. "Don't worry," I start. "I'll be—"

"I'll go grab my car," he states firmly with a smirk, turning on his heel and marching off across the parking lot.

I watch him go, torn between relief and embarrassment. If this works, then I could escape an expensive tow bill.

A few minutes later, Professor Henry drives over, parking his car in front of mine. I move between the two cars, grasping the front lid to lift the hood. Professor Henry moves behind me to do the same with his car.

I fiddle around for the latch under the hood lid, having a hard time finding it. After a few seconds, I finally hear the click, and then I start lifting. The hood is heavy, though—unlike modern cars, there's no automatic help hoisting it up into the air. I have to lift the entire dead weight of it.

I reposition my feet against the pavement under me to get better leverage, but as I do, my sneaker slams down into a puddle, and before I have time to correct, I've lost my footing, my shoe sliding against the slippery surface.

I try to steady myself but realize much too late that tumbling to the ground is inevitable.

To my surprise, strong arms wrap themselves around my waist, catching my fall and pulling me away as the hood of my car snaps shut with a bang.

I jump at the sound, still wrapped in Professor Henry's arms. Part of my t-shirt has ridden up my midriff, his forearm against my bare skin, sending fire through my veins. I freeze, barely able to breath, to move.

Professor Henry takes a step back, creating distance between us but still steadying me with his hands. "You okay?" he asks.

I turn to face him, his hands falling back to his sides. There's that same glint in his eyes again. That glint I'd seen last week in his office. Amusement.

"Yeah," I breathe. "Sorry."

He chuckles. "Let me lift the hood."

He brushes past me, and my body ignites where our arms touch briefly. He lifts the hood of my car, propping it up with the lever inside. I watch as he pulls out his jumper cables, setting them up in each of the vehicles.

He's pushed up his shirtsleeves, revealing a few inches of his forearms, and I find myself staring at them as he works. I swallow. God, it's unfair for someone to be this hot.

"So, bad at biology *and* cars?" he asks as he leans over my battery.

My mouth opens in shock, and I see him glancing at me with a smirk. An incredulous laugh escapes me. "We all have our weaknesses," I shoot back.

He chuckles. "Not so much of a genius, are we?"

"I never claimed to be a genius," I remind him. "You called me that."

He grins. "So I did."

Finished setting up the clamps, he returns to his car, turning it on. The engine rumbles to life. He gets out then gestures to my car. "Try to start it," he says.

I hop in, putting in the key and turning. It rumbles quietly for a second but then dies. I shoot him a grimace through the window.

"Try again!" he calls.

I do, and to my amazement, this time, it turns on. I stare down at the car in glee. "Yes!" I cry, jumping out of the car.

Grinning, Professor Henry moves to unhook the clamps, putting them back in his car.

"Thank you so much," I say. "Really. You saved me a huge towing bill." I laugh.

He smiles. "No problem." He waves off my gratitude.

We stand in silence for a heartbeat, the rumbling sound of my car's engine the only thing filling the silence.

"See you in class on Friday," he finally says.

I smile softly. "See you."

As that, he makes his way back to his car. I hop into my own, shutting the door and putting the car into drive.

Chapter 4

Kayla stares at me with wide eyes. "Your hot biology professor *came to your rescue*?"

Tossing my car keys on the counter in our apartment, I roll my eyes, laughing. "Okay, it's not that dramatic." Although, thinking about how he'd caught me mid-air while trying to open my hood does sound pretty dramatic. Not to mention the things my heart was doing when his arm brushed my bare stomach.

But Kayla doesn't need to know about that.

She shoots me a suspicious look. "Sounds pretty dramatic to me. Seems pretty much any girl on campus would love to be in your shoes." She giggles.

I snort. "It *was* nice, okay?" I admit, to which she cackles in glee.

"Of course it was," she says. "Much better than a tow."

"So much better," I agree. "Now if I can only pass his class."

"How's that going, by the way?" she asks.

I walk to the fridge, pulling out a sparkling water, and then take a seat next to her on the couch. "Good, I think. Hopefully." I shrug. "I've been doing tutoring the last week and hopefully that helps."

"Good. Oh, by the way," she says. "Matt and I are taking a quick trip to Olympia this weekend," she tells me. "It's his dad's birthday so we want to surprise him."

"That sounds fun," I say. Matt and Kayla started dating freshman year, and it was evident pretty early on that they were it for each other. While I'd hoped for some fun party nights out on the town, as single girls, during our college experience, Kayla was definitely more relationship-oriented. Which, to be fair, I can't blame her for. If I could find a guy to stick around, I wouldn't complain. Most of my sex life has been one-night stands or month-long flings. As much as I wanted a boyfriend—both in high school and early college—I could just never manage one. They tended to just want to have some fun and move on.

So, instead of bumming myself out over it, I simply accepted it. I decided to have my fun too. Why search for a relationship if it's just not in the cards? Although sometimes witnessing Kayla and Matt's relationship can sting just a bit. But I don't usually let those moments linger.

"Yeah," Kayla agrees. "You'll get the apartment all to yourself."

"I'll be sure to throw a rager," I joke.

She laughs. After a few moments of discussing our upcoming weekend and my plans to study for my biology class, she launches into a story about one of her own classes. A Russian lit class that's kicking her butt. I'd much rather deal with Russian lit than biology, but I can see how it could be … monotonous.

"And you know what else would make that class less terrible?" Kayla asks me.

"What?" I ask.

"A hot professor."

I giggle.

Chapter 5

We get our latest exams back today.

I've been fidgeting in my seat all class in anticipation for this grade. I'd studied hard all week. I'd spent countless hours with the tutor. I'd gone over those flashcards a thousand times. I needed to start turning my grade around now in order to pass by the end of the semester.

And this was going to be my first decent grade. I just knew it.

I can barely pay attention as Professor Henry goes over our newest material. I notice him glancing at me throughout class. The vain part of me thinks back to our run-in in the parking lot. How he'd caught me, helped me with my car, and teased me about being a genius. But the rational part of me keeps pushing that aside. There is no attraction here.

Well. There might be, but it's definitely one-sided.

Suddenly, Professor Henry clears his throat. He reaches for a stack of papers on his desk, straightening them in his hands. "I have your exam results here," he announces. "While most did well, a few of you might be disappointed with your grade." Am I crazy, or does his gaze linger on me as he says that last part? My heart skips a beat. While I hadn't felt incredibly confident during the exam, I hoped I'd done better than usual. I cross my fingers as he goes down each row, handing out papers.

When he gets to my desk, his gaze lingers on me for a second too long. I look up, and our eyes meet. Is that disappointment I see, or something else? He sets the paper face down on my desk and moves on.

I take a deep breath and turn it over. My heart sinks. A "D." Shit. I suck air in through my teeth. I needed this exam to pass. At this point, are there even enough assignments to make up for it?

Panic sets in. Am I going to be able to graduate? Holy shit.

My graduation, my job after college, all flash before my eyes, disintegrating behind this failing exam in my hands.

"You're free to go," Professor Henry's voice pierces through my blurry thoughts, but my focus is still on the "D" scrawled at the top of my page. "Remember to keep up with the class readings."

Chairs squeak and shoes scuffle around me. I feel my fellow students brushing past, making their way out the door. When I finally come to my senses, I realize there's only a handful of us left in the room. I stuff my exam into my backpack and stand. I walk slowly up the aisle of desks, and when I reach the front of the room, Professor Henry's gaze meets mine.

"Violet?" he asks, his facing falling. "You alright?"

I nod, hearing the last remaining students exit through the door behind me. "Yeah," I lie. "I just …" I trail off.

He grimaces knowingly. "I wish I could have given you a better grade." He looks like he means it. He really does. Which means I probably did worse than I think.

Embarrassment courses through me. Shit.

"I need to pass this class," I say. I stare down at my exam in defeat. "I'm supposed to graduate in May," I tell him. "And I need to pass this." I stare at him desperately, and his expression is one of compassion and concern.

He comes around from behind his desk, passes in front of me—his shirt sleeve brushing my arm—and sits casually against the front of his desk. He's a mere foot from me. And even though he's technically sitting, he still towers over me.

"How has the tutoring been going?" he asks.

"Not good enough, apparently," I mutter in frustration.

He reaches out to hold my forearm comfortingly, and I'm startled by the touch. Electricity courses through me.

"It'll be okay," he says reassuringly. I think he's going to remove his hand after his comment, but surprisingly he doesn't. It lingers, his thumb beginning to caress the bare skin on my wrist. I stare down at it, mesmerized.

When I glance back up to meet his gaze, there's an intensity there I haven't seen before. His eyes seem darker, somehow. After seconds of looking into those deep eyes, I forget how to breathe.

All of a sudden, he stands, and I think he's going to retreat to the safety behind his desk, but he doesn't. Instead, he takes a step impossibly closer to me, then moves so he's standing behind me.

He's standing so close that I can feel his breath on my neck. And just as I'm trying to chase away the thoughts of impropriety—that he's not actually coming on to me, that he's not actually into me—his hands brush my waist.

"There might be another way to make up your grade," he says softly.

My mind goes blank. "What?" is all I can manage to stutter.

Professor Henry moves back so that he's standing in front of me again, leveling me with his gaze. "If I've misjudged any ... *tension* between us as something different than what it is, then by all means, reject my offer," he starts. "But if not, I'd be willing to trade a passing grade for ... a time I think both of us would enjoy."

I continue to stare at him blankly until, all of a sudden, everything clicks into place. What he's proposing. My mouth drops open in shock.

Holy shit.

Professor Henry wants me to sleep with him in exchange for a passing grade.

I should be horrified. I should be offended. I should want to slap him across the face and storm out of here right now.

But, to my shock, I don't. To my shock, I ... am actually considering this?

No. No, no, no.

Holy shit. What am I doing?

"I want to be clear that refusing this will in no way impact your grade or our future professor-student relationship negatively," Professor Henry states seriously. "I only offered it because I suspect it's something you'd want as well. But if I'm wrong, I'll simply slink away to lick my wounds," he says with a smirk. He's giving me an out. A wide-open door for me to walk through. But the glint in his eyes tells me he knows he isn't wrong. Whether I take him up on this offer or not, he knows that sex with him isn't something I'd abhor.

"And if you'd rather," he continues, cocking his head with a soft smile. "I can try to find you a better tutor and more extensive study notes."

The door is getting wider. He's not trapping me. In fact, it's almost as if he wants me to go. He wants me to go if *I want* to go.

"It's just that my proposal would be so much easier." He smirks.

Fuck. He's right. It would be. With a huge final project for my main English class, as well as getting everything ready for my new job, spending hours every day studying biology is a huge drain on my time.

But … sleeping with my professor? Holy hell, do people even do this?

"Think about it," Professor Henry says. "I'm willing to help in whatever way you want. And if you want to take the genius route," he says with a playful smile, "I'll be happy to help you find a suitable tutor."

And with that, he turns back to his desk, grabbing his briefcase and papers, and walks out the door.

Chapter 6

I spend the weekend in a daze. I still can't believe that Professor Henry proposed what he did. And regardless of how terrible it sounds, and how the rational part of my brain had immediately rejected it, it didn't stop me from going home that evening and fantasizing about what it would be like to be with him.

His strong arms wrapped around me, his hands roaming across my body, his breath hot against my skin.

Fuck.

And he'd given me an out. An out so big it would be stupid not to take it. The only reason I'd take him up on his actual offer is because I truly want to do it. And that's what he wanted. For me to do what I want.

God, it only makes him hotter. When, in reality, I should be thinking of him as a creepy professor trying to sleep with his student. Although, as hard as I try, I just can't create the image. The only thing I can think of is how hot it *would* be to sleep with him.

On Sunday morning, I roll out of bed, still unsure of my decision. I hop into the shower, rubbing sleep from my eyes.

As I lather up the soap, my mind wanders to Professor Henry, as it has all weekend. I close my eyes, running my soapy hands along my legs, up my stomach, over my breasts. Imagining my hands are his, I sigh.

Electricity jolts through my stomach. The warm water cascades over my skin, washing away the soap. I reach lower, finding my slit and running my finger along it. Reaching my clit, I begin rubbing.

I think of Professor Henry, imagining him here, behind me, his hands wrapped around my stomach, his finger dancing across my clit. His breath warm on my neck, he'd moan softly, while his other hand would reach for my breast, massaging it.

The pleasure builds within me as I pick up speed, rubbing my clit faster.

Fuck, I'm close.

I imagine him murmuring in my ear, whispering my name. *Violet*. I remember how he'd said it in his office. With a tinge of amusement, a tinge of power, of dominance. *Violet*.

Or orgasm washes through me, and I gasp, reaching out to steady myself against the shower wall. Panting, I open my eyes, and a feeling of assurance settles over me.

Fuck.

Chapter 7

I can barely sit still during Professor Henry's class on Monday. I fidget in my seat, changing positions, glancing around, readjusting my arms and hands. It's as if my entire body is on fire and I have no way of putting it out.

I'd reasoned with myself all weekend. Went over all the pros and cons. And I'd settled on an answer.

I need this class to graduate. I need to pass it. There's no way around it. If I don't pass this class, I don't graduate, and I can kiss my amazing job opportunity goodbye. And I can't risk that.

I barely have the time to finish all my English class assignments—the ones that really matter to my future—much less spend *more* time with a tutor. I've always considered myself smart, but as time goes by and I try harder and harder, I'm just losing faith in myself. What if I truly can't pass this class on my own? What if I'm just not cut out for science? Maybe I truly can't do it. The idea is both frustrating and terrifying, but with graduation looming, I can't dwell on it.

And I've been presented with a golden opportunity. An opportunity that, in all honesty, would not be terrible.

It's not like I hadn't fantasized about Professor Henry before. Who hasn't? Like Kayla said, being saved by him in the parking lot last week is probably every female student's fantasy.

And I have the opportunity to sleep with him. Not only will I get a passing grade, but I get to sleep with Professor Henry. A fucking win-win if I ever saw one.

Professor Henry has been shooting me looks during the entire class. Not a look long enough for anyone to notice, but it lingers enough that I do.

"Remember the quiz next week," Professor Henry says as the clock strikes three. "And stay up to date on readings in the textbook."

The sounds of shuffling overtake the room as students grab their things and hurriedly exit. I pretend to fiddle around with something in my desk, waiting for everyone to leave. When they finally do, I stand, pulling my backpack with me.

Professor Henry is standing at the front of the classroom, watching me, waiting. His intense gaze lands on me, heavy.

Taking in a stuttering breath, I walk down the aisle of desks until I'm standing in front of him. "I thought about what you offered," I say, breaking the silence.

He nods.

"I … think I'll take you up on it." Even though I'd already decided, the finality of my words lay heavy in the air. I've agreed. I'm going to do it.

A soft smile spreads across Professor Henry's face. He reaches out to gingerly brush a strand of hair behind my ear, then he trails his fingers down my jaw, gently holding my chin between them and lifting my face to meet his gaze. The gesture sends a fire starting in my lower belly.

His gaze darkens as he stares down at me. "There's one more thing you should know before you agree. About our arrangement."

I wait.

"I enjoy … the more dominant way of doing things," he states. "Can you handle that?"

My eyes widen slightly, but I find myself nodding. If I'm honest, I'm curious to find out what that means. What a *dominant* Professor Henry is like. He already seems pretty dominant to me.

"And I want you for the rest of the semester."

A continuing situation. Not just once. I take a second to process it. Surprisingly, it doesn't really change my feelings. Sleeping with him once vs. multiple times? I honestly don't see much of difference, personally. It's not like I was going to hate sleeping with him. I can't imagine that.

After a few heartbeats, I swallow. "Okay," I say.

He removes his hand from my chin.

"We'll ... sleep together. Until the end of the schoolyear," I say. "And you'll give me a passing grade." A jolt of electricity courses through me. I can't believe I'm doing this. But instead of dread or fear or shame, I feel ... excitement. Arousal? What I'm doing is deliciously dirty, and I can't help but crave it.

A smile spreads across Professor Henry's face. "That's the deal," he says.

I nod, letting out a shaky breath.

The deal. We've made the deal.

Holy shit.

Butterflies dance in my stomach, twirling together in an intoxicating sensation that's only intensifying by the moment.

Professor Henry takes a slow step toward me. Closing the distance between us, he places a hand on my waist, his mouth drawing close to my ear. "Want to officially seal the deal?" he whispers.

His hot breath on my neck sends shivers down my spine, and my eyes flutter. I sigh quietly. "Yes," I find myself answering.

He moves behind me, slowing brushing his hands along my waist. My breath catches in my throat as he pulls me back against him. Holy shit. Is this really happening?

His hands travel slowly up my stomach, above my clothes, over my breasts. His thumb lingers, caressing its way across the tip of my breast—and suddenly he pinches my nipple through the fabric.

I let out a small squeal of surprise.

"That hurt?" he asks me, his lips caressing my ear.

"A little," I admit, shocked.

"Good," he says, then pinches the other nipple, sending another startled breath from my lips. "Because you've been a bad student. A bad girl."

My mouth drops open in shock. Holy fuck. A *bad girl*. Suddenly I understand what he meant by dominant. "Yeah," I breathe.

He pulls me tighter against his chest, his breath tingling against my neck, my ear. "I think there might be a way for you to make up for it though."

I swallow. I turn my head to the side, even though he's too close for me to really look at him.

"Think of it as super fun extra credit." He chuckles softly. His hand slides under my shirt, his fingers cool against the skin of my stomach. His fingers explore, up, up, up, under my bra. I shudder as he twirls circles around my breast, increasingly closer to the center, but never touching it. "Are you up for some extra credit, Violet?" he whispers in my ear.

Oh god, the way he's touching me. I arch my back, waiting for him to touch my nipple, but he refuses my body's request.

"Well?" he prompts.

"Yes," I breathe. "Yes."

He continues his patient swirls. "Good. Here are the rules."

I'm nodding, ready to accept whatever they are.

"I get to do whatever I want to you."

My mind momentarily halts. Whatever he wants? *Whatever* he wants? What does that mean? What exactly does he want? But his finger is inching closer and closer to the center of my breast, and this train of thought is getting harder and harder to keep on track.

"Violet?" he prompts in that wicked-deep whisper. He flicks my nipple, sending me into a blinding second of ecstasy, and a small whimper escapes me. "Is that a yes?"

His thumb gently caresses my nipple, and I nod. "Yes, okay. I agree."

His wandering hand halts. "Good." I can hear the smile in his voice. And suddenly his hands are gone, and I feel his body moving away from me.

I turn, the sudden loss of his touch jarring. I watch as he marches to the door, pulls the blinds over the small window, and turns the lock on the knob.

And now, with his lack of touch, with the door locked, and my mind finally thinking straight again, doubt begins to creep in. What have I agreed to?

To let your hot-as-fuck biology professor have his absolute way with you, Violet, that's what. Verbalizing it in my mind makes me instantly wet. Fuck. This is really happening. I'm about to get absolutely fucked by Professor Henry.

He turns to look at me, and I already feel naked under his intense stare. He's still standing by the door, fifteen feet away, and yet I feel like a trapped bird in a cage. With a cat that's ready to pounce. He stalks toward me, slowly.

Butterflies battle in my lower stomach. Is that excitement or fear? I'm really not sure.

Professor Henry stops two feet away from me, his gaze gliding up and down my body. "Are you going to be a good girl for me today, Violet?" he asks softly.

I nod.

"Use your words."

"Yes."

"Yes what?" he asks, his eyebrows raising.

"Yes, Professor Henry?" I guess, and his gaze softens in approval.

"Good girl, Violet."

51

My pussy clenches at the comment. *Good girl.* Fuck. God yeah, I want to be his good girl.

"Lie face up on my desk, Violet," he commands.

I'm shocked at his demand, but I hurry to do as he says, taking a deep breath. I hope I'm not shaking, not as outwardly nervous as I feel. I sit my butt down on his desk, sliding backward and then lying down, my knees dangling off the edge.

"Raise your arms above your head."

I do as I'm told.

Professor Henry disappears from my line of sight, and then I feel something tighten around my wrists. My eyes widen. Holy fuck. He's tying my wrists together above my head. I'm not sure with what. It feels soft. His tie, maybe? As the tension grows, I realize that he's also secured them to something else.

I'm tied down.

I take a deep breath. This is real. This is really real.

Professor Henry comes back into view, standing above me. He brushes a strand of hair from my face. "Violet, I'm going to have *so* much fun with you," he says, and it makes me even wetter.

And with that, he goes to the edge of the desk and kneels, removing my shoes and socks. I don't have tights on—only a skirt and underwear. His fingers slowly trail up my legs as he stands. I have half a second to wonder how exactly he's going to fully undress me with my wrists already tied down, when he leans over, grabs my shirt and bra and yanks them up over my breasts to sit at my collarbone, fully exposing me. I shudder at the rush of cold air, and my nipples harden. Then he reaches under my skirt, flips it up so he can see my underwear. He loops his fingers on either side of my hips and slides my panties down my legs.

And there I am, still technically clothed but somehow so, so exposed. It somehow makes it worse. To still have clothes on, yet in all the wrong places.

But just when I expected Professor Henry to go to town, to fuck me into oblivion, he steps back. He leans casually against his desk chair, cocking his head and devouring me with his gaze.

My breathing increases, somehow feeling more violated and uncovered with him five feet away, doing nothing. At least if he were fucking me, we'd *both* we doing something. But instead, I'm lying here, tied to his desk, my breasts and pussy on full display—alone.

"Professor?" I manage to ask, but it comes out in a breathy whisper.

He smirks. The silence stretches on, and with each second, I can feel myself becoming redder and redder. The humiliation burns through me. I've never let a man see me like this, and Professor Henry is just taking me in like I'm some buffet.

"God, I've wanted this for so long," he finally breaks the silence. He stands and stalks toward me. "And how could I not?" He reaches out to caress one of my breasts. It starts as a soft touch that ends with a sudden, sharp pinch.

I gasp.

"You've been such a bad girl, failing all my tests." He tsks. "Such a bad girl, Violet."

I nod.

"Are you sorry?" he asks.

I nod again. "I'm sorry, Professor Henry."

"How sorry?"

"So sorry, Professor Henry."

"Good girl."

There's that term again. My pussy clenches.

I'm shocked at the dirty talk, at the things he's saying, but what's even more shocking is how much I'm into it. And he *had* warned me. He'd said he liked being dominant. And I guess this is what he'd meant.

He moves to the edge of the desk and suddenly hoists my legs up so my feet are resting on the desk, then violently spreads my legs apart. He gazes down at my center, then looks back up at me. He grins. "You're already dripping," he purrs. He runs a hand from my knee, down my thigh, closer and closer. And then there it is, right at my entrance. He looks up and locks eyes with me as he slides one finger inside.

I gasp, arching my back. It's only one finger, and yet with the buildup of anticipation, it feels like heaven.

"You know, Violet," he says. "Every time you sit in this classroom now and look up at this desk, you're going to think of what I've done to you." He glances sideways at the rows of empty desks. "What you let me do to you." He curls his finger inside me, and I moan. "If only your classmates could see you now. Perfect, put-together Violet. Not so put together now, are we?" He smirks, and then, when I don't respond, repeats, "Are we?"

"No, Professor Henry," I cry quietly.

He pulls his finger from within me, and I sigh, relaxing against the desk.

"So eager," he commends.

My chest rises and falls with each heavy breath. I'm so turned on, it's crazy. The dirty talk, the fingering, the fact that anyone could walk in and see me like this—tied down, exposed, at Professor Henry's mercy.

"So eager," he repeats, his hand sliding back down my thigh. Only this time it ends at my clit, swirling small circles around my bud. I moan.

"You like that, sweetheart?"

"Yes," I breathe.

"Yes, what?" he asks, his voice hardening, pulling his hand away from my center.

I gasp at the lack of sensation.

"Yes, Professor Henry," I correct quickly. "Yes, Professor Henry."

"Good girl," he says, returning to the circles. He thumbs my clit, and I arch my back in pleasure. His circles become faster and faster, harder and harder, and I'm starting to see stars.

"Oh God," I cry. "Oh *God*."

But just as I'm about to fly over the edge, he stops.

The termination comes so abruptly, it almost hurts, and I cry out. I writhe, but Professor Henry roughly steadies my knees. "You'll cum when I want you to cum, Violet," he says softly. "Remember the agreement."

I nod, breathing heavily. "Yes, Professor."

He steps away, and I'm right back to being utterly, humiliatingly exposed again. Only it's worse this time, my wetness dripping all over my legs and the desk, my chest heaving from my almost-orgasm. I didn't think I could feel more humiliated, and yet here I am.

Professor Henry strides to the other end of the desk, where my head is. He strokes my hair, then leans down to my ear. "Your turn to please me, sweetheart."

He grabs my arms and pulls, sliding me toward him until my head hangs off the desk. He unzips his pants, and suddenly I'm faced with his cock. Literally. He strokes it a few times, and I'm immediately intimated by the size. Holy shit. Will that fit in me? Either end of me?

"Be a good girl, Violet," he says, guiding his cock to my mouth. I open and am immediately overwhelmed with his size. But there isn't anything I can do about it, tied to the desk, my neck pressed against the wood, unable to move. He thrusts deeper into my mouth, my throat, and tears spring to my eyes.

"That's a good girl," he says, his voice husky now.

He thrusts in and out, slowly at first, and I start to moan—both from discomfort and arousal. The fact that his dick barely fits, that it hurts against the back of my throat, is hot. He starts to pump faster and faster now, and I moan each time. His fingers play with my breasts, jiggling on full display above me. He pinches my nipples harder and harder, the pain turning me on even more.

"Good girl, sweetheart," he says, his voice tight with pleasure. He pinches both my nipples, hard, and I cry out in pain. I can feel his cock pulsing in my mouth, but instead of cumming like I think he's going to, he pulls out, his slick cock bouncing in front of me.

He disappears from view, and I'm left gasping, hanging over the edge of the desk. Then I feel his hands around my legs, pulling me back across the desk so that my knees hang off the other edge.

"And now I finally get to fuck your tight pussy," Professor Henry purrs, pushing my legs apart. He opens a drawer on his desk, pulling out his wallet, from which he procures a condom. I hear him tearing it open and sliding it on.

I feel his cock at my entrance, and nerves dance in my stomach. He barely fit in my mouth, and I'm worried about him fitting down there. But I don't have time to contemplate it before he's sliding into me.

I gasp at his size. My pussy stretches to accommodate it. "Good girl, Violet," he says, slowly pumping in and out of me. And now that I've relaxed around him, he feels—God, he feels like nothing I've ever felt before. As if he's splitting me open from the inside in the best way possible.

"You like that sweetheart?" he asks.

"Yes, Professor Henry," I moan.

He pumps faster now, angling to perfectly hit my sweet spot, causing me to cry out in pleasure with each thrust.

"You like my cock, sweetheart?"

"Yes, Professor."

He pumps faster and faster, his hands gripping my knees, his fingertips digging into my flesh. My moans are getting louder and louder, and I hope no one is out in the halls to hear, because I can't help myself. I'm on the verge of whimpering hysterically in pleasure, the tension building and building, when I feel Professor Henry's release inside me. He goes still for a moment and pulls out.

I watch as he nonchalantly pulls the condom off and tosses it in the trash, buttons up his pants, steps back, and takes a long, cool look at me.

I'm still breathing heavily, my body aching for an orgasm. And he knows it. He can see the pleading in my eyes. He smiles. "You were a bad girl, Violet. You don't get an orgasm."

Shocked, I whimper in protest, the only thing I can think to do. I'm desperate. I've never been this desperate. I writhe, pulling against the restraints on my wrists. But my naked body does nothing to tempt him. He's already fully satiated.

He comes closer. "Maybe next time, if you're a good girl, I'll let you cum."

My mind jolts. Fuck. Not only does he like to be dominant in how he speaks, but also in ways like this.

He scans my body again. "I do love seeing you like this. Maybe I'll just leave you here until class tomorrow morning. Let the other students know what a bad girl you've been."

I know he's bluffing, but the comment sends real fear coursing through my veins. The idea of those idiot freshman boys seeing me like this. Probably taking advantage of the situation and fucking me while they could.

"But I'd rather not share the sight." He smirks and walks to the edge of the desk, untying my restraints. I scramble up from the desk, pulling my shirt down and scanning the floor for my panties. I grab them and slide them on.

Professor Henry is already unlocking the door. I follow him there, and he turns to me. "Don't you want to thank me for the extra credit?" he asks.

I swallow. "Thank you for the extra credit, Professor Henry."

He smiles. "Good girl."

My whole body, still aching for the orgasm I was denied, buzzes with desire. Professor Henry opens the door, and I step out into the hallway.

"See you tomorrow, Violet. Don't be late." And with that, he shuts the door.

My breathing still ragged, I stand alone in the empty, dark hallway, shocked at what just happened. Professor Henry fucked me.

And ... I loved it.

The way he'd spoken to me, touched me, what he'd done to me. I'd never been fucked like that in my life.

The easiest A in my life, and all I can think about is doing it again.

Chapter 8

I see the new grade appear on my student dashboard almost immediately. A+.

It really happened. I really just had sex with my hot biology professor for an "A" in his class. I can't decide whether to be thrilled or disgusted. Am I really that kind of person? Oh my God …

I bury my head in my hands and turn away from my laptop. I am. I most definitely am. The A+ on my screen confirms it. At least I'll pass the class.

I sit in the silence of my room for a moment, waiting for the shame to hit me. The inevitable horror at what I've done.

But as the seconds tick by, it doesn't arrive. Strangely, I don't feel bad at all. I feel … incredible.

I just had the best sex of my life. And not only do I get an A out of it, but I get to do it again.

I glance around my room. I'm sitting at my desk in the corner, my laptop open on the surface in front of me. Suddenly, those hours I'd normally spend studying biology are no longer needed. I have time on my hands. A lot of it.

Kayla isn't due to be back from her dinner date with Matt for awhile, so I'll hold off on our ritual of reality TV watching until then.

A sudden curiosity grips me, and after a moment of hesitancy, I give in. I go online to Kensington University's website and click on professor profiles. It only takes me a second to find Professor Henry's. He looks just as attractive in his photo as he does in person. A gray suit with a deep blue tie. I skim his bio. Graduated with his PhD from UCLA and started his professorship position here just a few years ago. He's one of the youngest professors the university has ever had.

Further intrigued, I continue my search on Facebook, finding his personal profile easily. At first, it almost feels like a violation. His profile is public, meaning I can see pretty much everything. And it isn't tailored to his professional accomplishments. There are photos of him with family, with friends—his profile photo is one of him hiking.

But then that hesitancy vanishes when I remember what we've done. Any ounce of propriety I once held is no longer valid. So I keep going.

Finding his birth year, I find I was pretty accurate in guessing his age. He's twenty-nine. Perusing through his pictures, I see he enjoys hiking in the Seattle area. He also seems to have traveled a decent bit as well— there's a photo of him in front of Machu Picchu.

I also see some photos of him with kids. Two little boys. It takes me a few minutes to realize they must be his nephews—his brother's kids. There are tagged photos with him at birthday parties, as well as giving them piggyback rides and playing in a pool. It's adorable, actually. It makes the standoffish Professor Henry suddenly seem so much more human.

As I continue to scroll through his photos, something eventually snags my attention, sending my heart racing just a bit faster. I click on the image.

A photo of him and a woman, his arm around her. Their smiles are wide, and they're dressed nicely—at some kind of an event, perhaps. The woman is beautiful. Long, blonde hair, gorgeous blue eyes. She leans against Professor Henry, her hand resting against his chest as they grin for the photo. My eyes widen when they land on her hand. A delicate diamond ring is nestled there.

Oh my god.

I continue through his photos, finding only a handful of tagged photos of them. But in each one, they have their arms around each other, very obviously displaying affection.

I hurriedly scroll to his "about" section to check his official relationship status, suddenly terrified that I've just slept with an engaged or married man. But it reads "single."

I frown. Going back through the photos, I notice they're dated from three years ago. And they only show up in photos that he's tagged in, meaning any photos he posted himself of them have been scrubbed.

Was he engaged? And it ... failed? God. How awful.

I stare at another photo of them, blown away by how beautiful his former fiancée is. Suddenly, I feel self-conscious. I'm nothing compared to this elegant bombshell of a woman.

But then I snap myself out of it. *You're not dating him, Violet*, I remind myself. *You're just having sex. There's a huge difference.*

And I should know.

Meaningless sex is all I've ever had. I think back to my first time. I'd been eighteen, a freshman here at Kensington. Self-conscious about my lack of experience, I'd befriended a cute guy in one of my classes with the intention of sleeping with him. And it worked. It wasn't an incredible experience, but I was no longer a virgin. And from then on, all my sexual encounters were pretty similar. I'd go on a few dates with a guy, we'd sleep together, but eventually we'd drift apart—or, more accurately, he'd find a reason to dump me. Every once in awhile, I'd initiate a one-night stand via Tinder. And those could be fun.

But I think of Kayla and Matt sometimes. Their adorable date nights. One of which is happening right now. He'll bring her flowers, and I can't help but imagine what it would be like for a guy to bring me flowers.

Whatever. It doesn't matter.

I exit out of Professor Henry's Facebook page, tired of seeing him with that gorgeous blonde. At least he's not with anyone right now. I'd feel horribly guilty about sleeping with someone in any kind of relationship. I don't think I could do it.

Lucky for me, it seems our situation can continue.

Chapter 9

When I walk into Professor Henry's classroom the next day, it's like every nerve in my body is on fire. I purposefully avoid Professor Henry's gaze as I slink inside and race to the back of the classroom where I normally sit. I take my seat, head down.

I'm afraid if I lock eyes with him, somehow, everyone will know. My face will turn bright red, and my thoughts will be projected into the air above my head for everyone to read: *I had sex with Professor Henry. And we're definitely going to do it again.*

Students file in around me, chatting and sitting. I risk a glance up to find Professor Henry's gaze glued to me. That same intense, inscrutable look on his face.

My heart rate immediately spikes.

He leans against his desk, casually tapping the wood with his fingers, a smirk on his face, reminding me of what we did barely twenty-four hours ago. I take in the desk, remembering how he fucked me on it. The power of his thrusts, how his cock felt so big it almost hurt. I feel my face redden at the thought— that no one else in this classroom knows.

He finally breaks eye contact, clears his throat, and greets the class as a whole. He starts going over our latest chapter in the textbook, writing key points on the blackboard, then taking time to discuss and ask questions.

Every once in a while, his gaze darts to me and lingers just a bit too long. I'd think I was imagining it if it wasn't for what transpired yesterday. Is he thinking about what we did too? Replaying it over and over again in his mind? Thinking about what I looked like naked? What I let him do to me?

I swallow and take a deep breath, trying to focus on the lecture. But all I can think about is how deftly his fingers brought me closer and closer to—

Stop it, Violet. Focus. This chapter is just as boring as all the others have been, but I try my hardest not to fantasize and actually pay attention.

By the time class ends, I'm so restless I could burst. I hurry to gather my things into my backpack and follow the rest of the students out into the hall when I'm interrupted by a voice.

"Violet?" His deep tone stops me in my tracks. "Can I speak with you a minute?"

Just his voice sends a shiver down my spine, electricity at my core. I turn. "Yes, sure," I say as casually as I can, as the last few students file past me. The heavy door slams shut with an ominous bang, leaving us in the silence of an empty room.

Just us and the knowledge of what happened here.

"How are you?" he asks after a too-long heartbeat.

"I'm good," I answer. "Thank you for the improved grade."

He smiles slowly. "You're the one who did the extra credit."

My heart skips a beat. He's right, technically. I did.

His smile transforms slowly into an amused smirk. "You liked the extra credit, didn't you?"

"Yes."

"You mean it?" he asks, and while his demeanor doesn't change, I can somehow sense that he truly cares about my answer. Is concerned, possibly.

"I do," I say, truthfully. "I enjoyed it … Professor Henry." The last part comes as a whisper, afraid that we're dancing over ice so thin that any wrong word count break it.

But at my words, his smile deepens. "Good," he says, and it sounds like butter. "Would you … like more?"

The wetness at my core answers for me. Fuck, yes. Yes.

"Yes," I say, my voice almost too eager.

His eyes sparkle. "You did your extra credit well. You've been a good girl," he says. "And if you continue to be good, I'll let you ... have your reward."

The thought of my denied orgasm yesterday claws at the edge of my memory. And the idea of actually cumming at the hands of Professor Henry. My body can hardly wait.

"Strip," Professor Henry says.

I balk. "What?"

He raises an eyebrow. "You heard me. Take your clothes off."

My eyes dart to the door, the shades still drawn from yesterday, but the knob still very unlocked. "Aren't you going to—"

"No one tried to come in yesterday," he interrupts me. "So why bother?"

The idea terrifies me, and he knows it. He likes it. The danger of someone walking in. I hesitate, still looking at the door.

"Violet?" he asks. "What are you waiting for?"

I look back to him. I drop my backpack to the floor and slip out of my shoes. I pull off my top, unbutton my jeans, and slide out of them. I'm in my bra and panties, standing in the center of the room. A room that just minutes ago was filled with fellow classmates.

After a moment of silence, Professor Henry chuckles. "Everything," he clarifies.

My breath catches in my throat. I had assumed so, but standing in my underwear alone is terrifying enough. But as the seconds go by and his gaze hardens and hardens, I can't take it anymore. I reach behind me to unclasp my bra, letting my breasts spill out and the fabric fall to the floor. Then I slide my panties down my legs and step out of them. I stand there, breathing heavily from the nerves. Which is funny, because it's not like he hasn't already seen all there is to see of me.

"Good girl."

He walks slowly toward me, taking it all in. And I'm right back to yesterday, feeling so exposed I could die. The cold air hardens my nipples into pink, erect buds, practically begging to be plucked and teased. Professor Henry circles me, slowly.

"Do you think you deserve to cum today, Violet?" he asks.

It feels like a trick question. Damned if I do, damned it I don't. Or, fucked if I do, fucked if I don't. Which I guess is kind of the point.

"Answer me," he prompts.

"Yes," I say. And I do. I was good yesterday. I followed the rules. I let him do whatever he wanted, and I didn't protest. And I didn't get to cum yesterday, so I'm aching for it.

He comes to stand in front of me, eyeing me up and down. "Are you prepared to earn it?"

I nod.

He cocks his head. "Manners, Violet."

"Yes, Professor Henry."

"I'm going to make you earn your orgasm, and if you're a good girl, I'll let you cum," he says. "Okay?"

"Yes, Professor Henry."

He smiles. "Good. Now, kneel."

I sink to my knees, leaning back against my heels. I'm painfully aware of the unlocked door. How humiliating it would be to be found like this, naked and kneeling on the floor of my biology professor's classroom.

But I don't have time to dwell on it before Professor Henry is unzipping his pants and pulling out his cock. There's something wickedly dirty about how fully dressed he is, how naked I am, his cock inches from my face.

"Be a good girl and suck my cock," he instructs, tenderly brushing hair from my face before grabbing a fistful of it in his hand.

I barely have time to open my mouth before he's slamming his dick inside, pushing my head down around it. He pumps viciously, and my throat burns, and my eyes tear up. I moan in discomfort, but he keeps going.

"Good girl," he says softly. "Good girl, taking it like that."

I relax at his praise, feeling my pussy getting wet. I like that he's rough with me. That I'm nothing but his little whore, naked on the floor, being mouth fucked purely for his pleasure. The lack of control is freeing. Soon my moans of discomfort turn to moans of pleasure. The pleasure of being used and dominated.

His thrusts quicken and deepen, faster and faster. I anchor myself against his legs, clutching the backs of his thighs for dear life. "Such a good ... girl," he pants, his voice catching. "*So* good." I can hear the strain in his voice, the lack of composure, and it gets me even wetter. The fact that I'm doing this to him. That I'm making him feel this good.

And just as I feel his cock jerk and twitch, he pulls out, cumming all over my face and chest. His cum spills down my breasts, my stomach. I gasp in shock. He smiles down at me. "Good girl."

Then he turns so abruptly that I lose my balance and fall to all fours. He walks to the front of the room, leaving me a sticky mess on the floor. "I—" I stutter.

He walks to his desk, opening a drawer and pulling something out. "Follow me up here, Violet," he commands.

I stumble unsteadily to my feet and do as he says. When I reach him, I gesture to the box of tissues on his desk, then at me. "Can I ...?" I ask.

He gives a single shake of his head. "No."

I purse my lips, feeling his cum continue to slide down my bare skin. I thought kneeling naked was humiliating, but standing bare covered in Professor Henry's cum is a new level of shame.

Professor Henry straightens. "Sit," he orders, motioning to his desk chair.

I take a seat, and he immediately moves to stand behind me. And then I realize what he'd gotten from his desk. Ropes. He ties my hands behind my back through the bars of the chair. Then he comes around to the front, spreads my legs, and ties each ankle to its respective chair leg. When he's done, he stands back to observe his work.

He smiles. At me. Bare, tied to his chair, legs spread open, his cum still covering my neck and breasts.

"Do you think you were a good girl just now, Violet?" he asks.

I nod. "Yes, Professor Henry."

He cocks his head. "Why?"

I can't tell if this is a trap. If he's going to somehow swing it in his favor, tell me I was bad, and work me up, up, up again only to deny me what I truly want. But I *was* good. "I did exactly what you told me to," I say.

"And tell me what that was."

I take in a shuddering breath. "I sucked your cock, Professor Henry."

He nods in approval. "You did. And you did a good job."

I can't help but warm at his praise. I did a good job. I was good.

"What else?"

"I ... let you be rough with me."

He nods. "You did. That was very good. And the last thing?"

"I let you cum all over me, Professor Henry. And I'm still covered in it. I'm covered in ... your cum."

He smiles. "Yes, Violet. Good girl." He takes an antagonizingly slow step forward. "And you know what good girls get?" He braces one arm on an armchair, the other reaching out to caress my breast. I shiver at the touch. "What do they get, Violet?"

"Do they get to cum, Professor Henry?" I ask hopefully, arching my back into his touch.

He softly fingers my nipple between his thumb and forefinger. "Yes. So smart. Good girls get to cum. Do you want me to make you cum?"

I'm nodding before he's even done with his sentence. "Yes, Professor Henry. Please," I beg.

He grins his wicked grin and, while still fingering my nipple, leans down to take the other one in his mouth. I moan loudly, unable to stop myself. His tongue dances across my bud, first softly, then quicker, flicking it over and over. I arch my back, pressing closer against him.

He stops to look up at me. "Don't be greedy, Violet," he commands.

"I'm sorry, Professor," I say quickly. "I'm sorry."

He returns to my breast, his tongue swirling circles around my nipple, dancing closer and closer. He pinches the other with his other hand, causing a small shriek to erupt from my mouth.

Then his hand travels lower, down my abdomen, down my hip, until it's at my aching, wet entrance. He runs a finger along the folds, still tonguing my breast, and I gasp. He offers a soft bite as a parting gift, then leans back on his heels, directly in front of me.

He gazes down at my center, spread wide for him to see. "So pretty and wet for me," he compliments.

And with that, he inserts a finger. I resist the urge to arch my back, to buck toward him. Based on his last reaction, he might stop and chide me again. And I can't have that. I can't. All I can comprehend is more, more, more. I want all of him, inside me, all over me, wherever he wants.

He expertly finds my sweet spot, pushing up and curling his finger. And this time, I can't help myself. I buck my hips closer to him, moaning in pleasure.

He tsks but doesn't stop. "Normally, I'd ask you to restrain yourself, Violet. But you've been so good today. And this is your reward," he says.

I'm nodding, eyes closed, my head thrown back over the chair. I don't care what he says. I don't care what he does, as long as he keeps making me feel like this.

He adds another finger and starts pumping, slowly. I whimper, trying to move in rhythm with him, feel more of him, deeper. I open my eyes to see his gaze glued to me, taking me in, his eyes somehow even more intense than I've ever seen them. He keeps his gaze locked to mine and slowly lowers his head, his tongue meeting my clit.

A high-pitched whimper escapes my throat as his tongue draws lazy circles around my bud. He flicks it, hard and sharp, and it's all I can do not to scream. He's still pumping his two fingers in and out of me, curling them upward to hit my sweet spot. His tongue moves faster now too, a rhythm that's about to undo me. And he can see it. His gaze is locked on mine.

My mouth opens in ecstasy, but I can barely make a sound. *Oh, God.* Is this real? Professor Henry on his knees, eating me out, pleasuring me until I see stars? How is this happening?

"*Oh,*" I squeal. My body starts to squirm, and I writhe uncontrollably. "I'm going to come, Professor," I pant, my hips bucking.

And just as I say it, I do, crashing over the edge with a shriek.

I expect him to stop, and he does—momentarily. He lifts his face from my center, but replaces it with his hand, continuing the quick motion of his tongue.

I buck again, only this time, to make him stop. I shake my head, the feeling too sensitive. "It hurts," I tell him.

He shakes his head. "Be a good girl and take it," he says. "Trust me."

"It's too much, Professor Henry," I protest.

His gaze darkens. "I'll decide when it's too much."

I whimper in pain, my clit aching in overstimulation. I struggle against the restraints, but I can't get away. "*Please*," I beg. Only as the seconds tick by, his quick caress becomes more and more bearable. Pain mixed with pleasure, more intense than I've ever felt. I can't take it anymore, but I know Professor Henry won't stop. I'm powerless, at his mercy.

My hips buck without my consent. I'm moaning and whimpering in a pathetic, humiliating way I've never done before.

"That's it," Professor Henry praises.

I feel myself building up again, the discomfort only making it more intense.

"Look at me, Violet," Professor Henry orders. "Look at me when you cum."

I meet his gaze, nodding.

"Are you a good girl?" he asks.

I nod.

"Use your words."

"Yes, Professor Henry."

"Do you want me to make you cum for the second time?"

"Yes, Professor."

He raises an eyebrow. "You think you deserve it?"

"Yes!"

He grins. "Beg for it, Violet. Beg me for it."

I moan as he pumps his fingers in and out of me faster, his other hand circling my clit. "Please, Professor Henry."

"Please what?"

"Please make me cum," I sob, writhing.

I look into his eyes and crest the second orgasm, crying out in ecstasy as it comes faster and harder than the first. He removes his hands from me, and I throw my head back against the chair, gasping for air.

When I finally look up, I see Professor Henry has retrieved the box of tissues. He reaches out to wipe my neck. I'm still tied down, so I can't do it myself. He draws the tissue down my neck, across my breasts, cleaning the liquid from me. It's a surprisingly tender and intimate gesture. When he's done, he unties my ankles, then my wrists.

"It wasn't too tight?" he asks. The domineering tone is gone, replaced by a softer one.

I shake my head. "No."

"Good."

I remain seated as he fetches my clothes from across the room, bringing them back to place on my lap. "I have a meeting to catch, so I have to go," he says, grabbing a laptop bag from beside his desk. "Be a good girl and lock the door when you leave." He shoots me a soft smile, strides across the large classroom, and leaves.

I sit, stunned, for a moment, almost more uncertain around the softer, kinder Professor Henry of the last few minutes than of the man who roughed me up.

After a moment, I shake my head and hurriedly put on my clothes. I turn off the lights and lock the door as I leave. Just like Professor Henry ordered.

Chapter 10

The newest episode of *The Bachelor* plays on the TV while Kayla and I lounge on the couch. She's absentmindedly crocheting some new project while I fiddle around on my laptop.

"Can you believe graduation is only a month and a half away?" I ask her, opening an email from the college reminding us about our graduation gowns and dress attire.

She shoots me an excited look. "Right? It's crazy. I can't believe it."

A sudden sadness grips me. Kayla has already been accepted into a master's program a couple states away, which she'll be starting in the fall. And even though I knew it was coming—obviously we'd move on to other things after graduation—it makes me so sad to realize I won't be seeing her every day.

"It's kind of sad," I say.

She purses her lips. "I know," she admits. "The end of an era."

"Yeah," I agree. "What's Matt going to do?" I hadn't thought of it until now, but he must be pretty upset about her moving away as well. Would they do long distance?

Kayla grins. "He's looking for jobs in the LA area— near my school."

My eyes widen. "Oh wow. So he's moving with you?"

She nods enthusiastically. "Yeah!"

I'm not sure why this surprises me. I guess I knew they were serious, but I didn't realize how serious. I always assumed college relationships were just that.

College relationships that may or may not work out. But moving states away for someone? That's *serious*.

"So you'll be living together?" I assume.

She nods. "And …" She trails off, giving a somewhat embarrassed shrug. "I might feel dumb saying this but … I just have a feeling." She laughs. "I think he's going to propose soon."

My eyes widen even further. Propose? Holy shit.

"Oh my god," I stammer. "Kayla! That's … amazing."

She grins, her entire demeanor glowing. "I'm so excited, honestly," she says.

"Kayla," I repeat, leaning across the couch to give her a hug.

"I don't know for sure," she says, trying to wave me off with a laugh. "It's just a hunch."

"That's amazing," I repeat. It's the only word I can truly utter through my shock. Moving in together?

Getting engaged? God. I'm excited for Kayla, I really am, I'm just surprised. Her life seems to be taking such a serious turn. It's … all so much.

But I smile, seeing the joy emanating from her. "I'm happy for you," I say genuinely. "I really am."

Chapter 11

It's been a week since I last saw Professor Henry. Well, not since I last saw him. Since I last ... fucked him, I suppose. Or since *he* fucked me. I haven't had much agency in either of our sessions ... which, to be honest, I didn't really mind.

But I have technically *seen* him.

In class.

And that's it.

With graduation looming closer and closer, I've been preoccupied with getting everything together. Graduation attire, arranging travel plans for my family, preparing for my new job. It's all completely overwhelming and exciting at once.

But in the back of my mind, I keep going back to the sex I'd had with Professor Henry. The absolute hottest sex I've ever had—and I can't wait for it to happen again.

Only … am I supposed to wait for him to initiate? Am I supposed to … express interest first? Suddenly I feel like a nervous high schooler again, unsure how to approach my crush.

I lean back against my chair in the coffee shop, pulling out my laptop to check my newest homework assignments. When I log into the college portal, though, I notice a new grade notification.

Biology 101.

I bite my lip and click it. My mouth drops open.

An "F"?

I frown in shock. There's no way.

No fucking way.

Rage flushes through me. What the hell is he trying to pull? I sit in stunned silence for a moment, replaying everything. Is he afraid I'm going to tell someone about what we did? Is he trying to scare me? But what good would that do? If anything, it would make me more likely to tell someone.

In a moment of rash decision-making, I grab my stuff and storm out of my coffee shop. I make it across campus in a matter of minutes, marching into the biology department and scanning the room plaques for Professor Henry's office.

When I find it, I don't hesitate long enough to second guess my decision, grabbing the handle and jerking the door open.

"Professor—" My exclamation dies on my tongue as I see Professor Henry sitting calmly behind his desk, a student in the chair in front of him. He looks familiar. He's in my same Biology 101 class. "Oh," I stammer. "I'm sorry. I didn't mean to interrupt." My face feels flushed, and I start to back out of the room.

But Professor Henry stands. "No," he calls. "We were almost done." He glances to the student. "Levi, was there anything else?"

The student shakes his head, thanks Professor Henry, gets up, and slips past me out the door.

"I—" I begin. Professor Henry steps over to me, gently shutting the door. His gaze crashes over me, casually at first, but I see a fire deep within his eyes.

"Yes, Violet?" he asks.

I try to muster the rage I'd felt only minutes prior, but somehow it's difficult. "What—what's going on with my grade on that new test?" I demand. "Not only do we have our *arrangement*, but I did well. I know I did."

Professor Henry smiles and crosses his arms. "Do you, now?"

I frown. "I Googled some of the answers after I got the test back. You marked them incorrectly."

He raises an eyebrow. "Smart girl."

My frown deepens. "So what the hell? Why'd you do that?"

His gaze softens, and he takes a step closer, so close that I can smell his aftershave. Pine. He leans down to murmur in my ear, "Why do you think I gave you such a terrible grade, Violet?"

I shudder as his breath tickles my ear.

"Maybe so you'd come see me about it?" he finishes.

I jerk my head so that his eyes meet mine. So close. It's only now that I realize we've never kissed. Only … other things. I wonder what it's like to kiss him.

He shrugs. "I was never going to actually leave it like that."

I stand still for a moment, mouth open. "You …
wanted me to come see you?"

He nods slowly.

My stomach does summersaults at the
confirmation.

"But the fact that you jumped to such a conclusion
… that's not very good of you." His gaze darkens. "Plus
all those days after class this last week when you
scurried out of the classroom before I could even say
hello."

Heat pools between my legs. He thought I was
avoiding him? "It was a busy week," I stammer. And
it's true.

"What an excuse," he says, running his finger softly
up my bare arm, leaving goosebumps in his wake.
"Seems like you might need something to straighten
you out."

My mouth opens. Fuck. Whatever he has in mind, I'm down. In fact, I *need* it. He's right. It's been way too long since our last encounter.

"Do you think you need to be put in your place, Violet?" he asks, and his expression changes ever so slightly, and I know his question is deeper than what it seems. Am I okay with this? Do I really want to keep going? Want this to happen? Whatever this arrangement seems to be on the outside, what he truly wants is my permission. To make sure I'm enjoying this whole thing as much as he is.

And I know that I am.

I nod, my gaze still glued to his. "Yes, Professor."

He smiles. "Good." He glances to the door, then back to me. At first, I think he's going to take me right now, over his desk, and I'm wet at the thought, but instead he leans over, slowly. "Be in my office at 5 p.m."

I nod. "Yes."

"Yes what?"

"Yes, Professor Henry," I give in.

He smiles. "I'll see you then."

I scurry out of the classroom, my body already aching for what's to come. And already afraid of what it might entail.

■■■■■■■■■■■■■■■■■■■■■■■■■■■■■■■■■■■■■ ■ ı

I'm waiting in the hallway outside his office five minutes before 5, cracking my knuckles and crossing my legs in anticipation. He way he'd said *put me in my place* sends both anxiety and excitement dancing in my lower belly. What does that mean? Is his dominance, his rough handling of me only going to increase?

I should run. I should really go.

But I can't make myself leave. I'm undeniably drawn to him. Like a moth to a flame. A flame that does incredible things to my body and gives me feelings I've never felt before.

The door to Professor Henry's office opens abruptly, startling me.

"Come in, Violet."

I stand shakily and follow him into his office. He closes the door behind me and locks it, the click echoing in the silence of the room. He goes to sit at his desk, leaning back in his chair and staring at me. Seconds tick by in silence, and I'm becoming more and more uncomfortable. I shift from foot to foot.

"*Violet.*" The way he says my name sends shivers down my spine. I'm already wet. I was wet waiting for him in the hallway.

I swallow.

He smiles, and I know the game is on. "I can't let what you did go unaddressed. Ignoring me for a whole week and backtalking me today in my office."

I nod, wetter and wetter as the conversation continues.

He stares at me coolly for one moment longer, then commands, "Take your clothes off. All of them."

I do as he says, shedding my dress, bra, and panties.

He nods his approval. "Knees."

I sink to my knees.

He approaches me, and I assume he's going to have me suck his cock again, but instead I see ropes in his hands. He crouches behind me, tying my ankles together, then pulls my arms behind my back to tie my wrists. It's so tight it pulls my shoulders back, making my breasts more prominent than they normally are.

Then he stands and returns to his desk. To my shock, he sits down and opens his laptop.

"Professor?" I ask timidly.

He looks up at me, as if surprised I'm there. "Yes, Violet?"

"Are you …?"

"Am I what?" he asks. "Going to pleasure you?" He shakes his head. "No. You're going to kneel there on the floor, tied up and naked, while I finish my work for the day."

My mouth drops open, unable to speak. He shoots me a look, and I close it.

Professor Henry starts typing away, seemingly unaffected by the naked woman on the floor of his office. As the minutes tick by, I realize that he's completely serious. He wants me tied up on the floor while he does his work. He's actually working.

I bite back the disappointment, the frustration at not being touched. My body aches for him, my taut breasts practically reaching for his fingers. Why won't he touch me? Am I not desirable enough? What's more desirable than a fully nude woman tied up on the floor of your office? Completely at your mercy?

Fuck me, I want to beg but know better. He'd just use it as an excuse to wait longer.

I watch the clock on the wall out of the corner of my eye. Half an hour rolls by, then a full hour. My limbs are becoming stiff.

Suddenly, the desk chair scrapes against the floor, and Professor Henry stands. I look up at him hopefully.

He walks slowly over to me and without saying a word, unzips his pants and pulls out his already hard cock. Grabbing a fistful of my hair, he shoves his dick into my mouth. I grunt in surprise, then he starts pumping. I lean into it, but with my hands tied, I'm unable to brace myself on anything but his enormous cock at the back of my throat. I gag, tears streaming down my cheeks. While he's been rough the other times, this is rougher. I whimper in discomfort as more tears stream down my face.

"You've been bad, Violet," Professor Henry reminds me. "This is all about me and my pleasure right now." He continues thrusting until he empties inside of me, keeping his dick in my mouth as it fills with his liquid. He looks down to meet my gaze. "Swallow," he orders.

I do as I'm told, swallowing his cum. Some of it drips down my chin as he pulls his cock free. He leans down to wipe it away with his finger.

"Are you going to thank me for letting you suck my cock?"

"Thank you, Professor Henry," I say.

"For what?" he prompts.

"Thank you for letting me suck your cock."

He smiles. "Good girl, Violet."

My pussy clenches at the comment, even more desperate for him after he released himself in me. But instead of being a gracious lover and returning the favor, he instead returns to his desk, back to his laptop.

Another half hour goes by, and he somehow seems to be able to get work done despite the circumstances. The room gets colder as the sun sets outside, and my bare body isn't helping. I shiver, my nipples permanently hard now.

Professor Henry looks up every once in a while to rake his gaze over me. He does it lazily, taking me in. But he always goes back to his work.

At the second hour mark, he stands again, and a burst of adrenaline courses through me. He comes to stand near me and orders, "Lean forward."

I do, but he pushes me all the way down to the ground so that my chest and face are pressed to the linoleum floor, my hands still tied behind my back, and my ass in the air. He moves behind me, kneels, and I hear the unzipping of his pants again. I hear the ripping of a condom packet, and before I have time to prepare myself, he's inside me.

I'm not even wet, after an hour of sitting on the floor, so his cock sends a burst of pain through me as he enters. I shriek in protest, but Professor Henry slaps my ass so hard it silences me.

"Quiet, Violet." His tone is hard. "Remember, you were bad, and this is what bad girls get."

I whimper in response.

"Use your words. Tell me you understand."

"Yes, Professor Henry. I understand," I mutter into the floor.

"Tell me you deserve this. That you were bad."

"I was a bad girl, Professor. I deserve this," I repeat obediently.

"Good."

He continues thrusting, my pussy aching at his size. It feels like he's splitting me open. He grabs my hips to steady himself, pumping in and out of me. I rock against the floor to the rhythm of his thrusts, unable to brace myself with anything but my face and chest.

It doesn't take him long to finish, sliding out of me when he's done and returning to his desk without a word.

I struggle back to a kneeling position, my ankles and wrists still tied. My body aches from the stimulation but no orgasm. I'm turned on, but unable to do anything. I can't even touch myself. Not that he'd let me even if I could. I'm sure it would make me a bad girl in his eyes.

But as frustrating as this is, I can't deny that this the hottest encounter I've ever had. Tied up, at his mercy, on the floor of his office? I'm—shockingly—having the time of my life.

And he knows it.

I wait patiently as the minutes turn to hours. My body aches both from desire and from discomfort. I've been on the floor for hours at this point, and Professor Henry just keeps working.

"Professor?" I summon the courage to say.

He looks up with a questioning glance.

"I … my legs hurt," I stammer.

"Good." He goes back to his laptop.

"I'm cold," I venture.

"Good."

I bite my lip and go back to silence, determined to accept my faith. I will kneel here for as long as he pleases, and that's that. There's nothing I can do about it.

Eventually he gets up again, and I perk up. He comes to stand before me, looking down at my kneeling form. I know he can see the desire in my eyes, the begging.

He gives me a small smile then slowly reaches out to massage one of my breasts. It's the first act of pleasure specifically for me, and I melt at the touch. I throw my head back as he rolls my nipple between his fingers. His other hand follows suit with my other breast, and I moan.

"I know this is supposed to be your punishment," he says, "but I do love playing with your tits."

I arch, pushing my breasts closer to him, begging for more. He rolls my nipples faster, and I rock back and forth. He pinches just a bit harder, sending both pain and pleasure coursing through me.

"Tell me what you want, Violet," he commands.

"More, Professor," I say. "Please."

He crouches before me, and one of his hands moves to my clit. I gasp when he reaches it, twirling circles around it. He speeds up, faster and faster, and my hips start bucking. I moan loudly, feeling myself getting closer and closer.

But all of a sudden, he pulls his hands back.

I gasp, reeling forward from the lack of touch. I almost lose balance and fall on my face but manage to steady myself. Professor Henry stands, looking down at me.

"Wait," I stammer. "I wasn't—"

"I know you weren't done," he says. And with that, he returns to his desk.

No, no. I can't. I need the release. "Please," I say.

"No begging unless I tell you to," he replies.

I sink back onto my heels in frustration. I thought I wanted the punishment, but this is torture. To use me simply to please himself, then to work me up but not let me cum? It's sadistic.

It's a full half hour later when he returns to stand in front of me. I stare up at him, stoic.

"Lay on your back," he says.

I do as he commands, lying on my back, on top of my tied wrists, spreading my legs, still tied at the ankles, out wide. He gazes down at me. Then he kneels.

Keeping eye contact, he reaches out to massage my entrance, dancing up to my clit, then down again. I sigh in pleasure. He inserts a finger into me, then another, and another. He starts pumping, angling perfectly to hit my sweet spot.

I moan, writhing.

"Quiet, Violet," he warns.

But he keeps fingering my g spot, hitting it perfectly again and again with each thrust, and I can't help myself. I cry out in pleasure.

"I said, quiet," he says, and suddenly reaches up to slap one of my breasts, hard.

I gasp at the pain, my breast jiggling, red from the slap.

"I'm sorry, Professor," I say, somehow even wetter at this display of dominance.

He continues his finger thrusts, his other hand playing with my clit. Again, I feel the pressure building inside me, the edge coming closer and closer.

And then Professor Henry pulls his hands back.

I cry out in frustration, anger, want. "Professor!" I writhe, the pressure from the denied orgasm so intense it's unbearable.

"This is your punishment, Violet," he says again, slowly. "You don't get to cum today."

He moves to sit by my side and rolls me over so I'm on my stomach. I feel him untying the rope from around my wrists and ankles. "You're free to leave," he says, standing.

I scramble over to my hands and knees. No. I can't leave. I can't leave like this. After hours of teasing me?

"Please, Professor," I whimper from the floor.

"What did I say about begging?"

He's right. He told me not to. And denying him again could only make him angrier. But I can't help myself. I can't. I need his touch. I need to orgasm.

I do the only thing I can think to do, and I crawl across the floor on hands and knees toward him. He watches me coolly. I reach his feet and grip his pant leg, looking up at him.

"Please," I whisper. "I need it. Please."

He looks me over slowly for a moment that stretches into eternity, and just as I think he's going to tell me to leave, to pull myself together and not beg, something shifts in his eyes.

In a flash, he leans down and pushes me back against the floor. Kneeling over me, he unzips his pants, pulling his cock free. He grabs my hips and pulls me toward him, his cock meeting my entrance and sliding inside. I cry out in relief.

He climbs on top of me, grabbing both my hands and holding them down above my head. With the other hand, he covers my mouth. And then he fucks me. Hard.

I whimper under his hand, my moans muffled. His cock hits my sweet spot over and over, and I can feel the pressure building up inside me. The pressure that's been building for hours. I need this. I need this more than anything.

My whimpers have become hysterical at the pleasure building in my pussy. I writhe underneath him, but Professor Henry is strong, holding me in place.

"Should I let you come, Violet?" he asks, removing his hand from my mouth so I can speak.

"Yes!" I beg.

"Have you learned your lesson today?"

I'm nodding. "Yes, yes, Professor."

"You'll do as I say from now on?"

"Yes, yes, anything you say. Anything, Professor Henry." I can barely register the words coming out of my mouth. I'd promise him the moon if it meant that this pleasure never came to an end.

"Good girl."

And with that, he lowers his hand to my clit, painting furious circles.

I cry out, bucking against him. I open my eyes to see his face above me, and our gazes meet. I can tell he's close to orgasm, and I am too. I stare deep into his eyes, lost in the pleasure, lost in him.

I practically scream as I orgasm, the sound mixing with his deep moan of climax. His mouth opens in ecstasy. We lay like this for a moment, silent, spent. So long that I think he might lean down and kiss me. Like a normal couple would.

But after a moment, he stands, pulling himself from within me.

He watches me dress. "You were a good girl today, Violet."

And even though this evening was pure torture, the ending was worth it. His praise was worth it. I turn to him and smile. "Thank you, Professor."

Chapter 12

There's a raw ache between my legs from the events of yesterday. After Professor Henry tied my hands and legs, left me on the floor of his office, naked, and fucked me into oblivion. Twice. It's almost a pleasant sensation. The reminder of him. How he held me down, made me do exactly what he wanted …

My heart races at just the thought.

And a twinge of humiliation surfaces too.

It's late in the day—almost five. Most classes are done, but I'm hoping to catch him in his office. After all, he was here late last night. Although, he had more on his plate than I'm sure he normally does.

When I reach his office door, nervous butterflies dance in my stomach as I raise my hand and knock. A few tense seconds tick by before I hear a gruff, "Come in!"

I open the door to see Professor Henry sitting at his desk, consumed by his laptop. He looks up, and when our eyes meet, something soft yet harsh glitters across his face.

"Violet," he says. It's a statement meant to be devoid of emotion, but I can tell he's happy to see me. "You're back."

I nod. "I thought instead of waiting another week to come see you …" I start, my voice coming out less confident and sexy than I'd hoped. "I'd come … see you today."

An aura of approval settles over his features, and at the sight of it, my whole body warms. All I want is for him to call me good and reward me. The things he's done in the past are …

I shake my head, trying to force myself to focus on the here and now.

Professor Henry stands slowly and makes his way across the room. He stops a few feet from me, smiling down at me. "So, you did learn your lesson?"

I nod, swallowing.

"And you're going to be good for me from now on?" he prompts.

I nod again.

"Good." He reaches out a hand to caress a lock of hair from my face. I shiver in anticipation at his touch.

He turns away from me and goes back to his desk, scribbling something down on a bright orange sticky note. He returns, pressing it into the palm of my hand. "Meet me at this address in an hour." And with that, he opens the door to his office.

I barely have time to drop off my backpack at my apartment, shower, and reapply my makeup before getting in my car and plugging the address into Google Maps. It's only a ten-minute drive, but I don't want to be late.

The address is in a residential neighborhood near campus. The houses are mid-sized and uniform. Very suburban. And confirming my suspicions, I assume he must live here. I don't know why, but I'd always imagined him in an apartment. A nice apartment. Downtown. A bachelor pad. Something about him in an actual house makes him seem … more human? Normal? I'm not even sure.

I park on the street and make my way to the front door, double checking the address numbers to make sure it's the right one. Once I knock, I hear footsteps on the other side, and soon the door opens, revealing Professor Henry.

He smiles at me. "Come in, Violet."

He's dressed differently. No longer wearing the slacks and button ups I'm used to seeing him in, he's currently donning a gray t-shirt and sweatpants. On anyone else, it would make him seem less intimidating—but somehow, he still commands the room.

He leads me to the living room, and I'm surprised at the space. How nicely decorated it is. Still masculine, yet neat. Bookshelves line the walls, and a small fireplace burns in the corner.

"You live here ... alone?" I ask, almost wondering if the decoration is thanks to a woman's touch. The blonde woman from the Facebook photos, perhaps? The thought makes my skin crawl with jealousy. Not that we're *dating*. But the idea of him doing what he does to me to someone else is ... upsetting.

As always, he seems to pick up on my thoughts and simply answers, "Yes, just me," with a small smile.

I relax a bit at that.

"Do you want something to drink?" he asks.

I'm surprised at the offer, but I nod. He exits the room to where I imagine a kitchen must be. I continue looking around, almost more nervous than I've been other times around him. This just feels different. Him offering me a drink? Like this is some kind of date? Me meeting him at his house? It's all so much more … intimate.

He returns with two glasses of wine, handing me one.

I drink half of it way too quickly, my nerves obviously getting the better of me. He notices and motions for us to sit on the couch. "Are you nervous, Violet?" he asks, his tone amused but also a little concerned.

I shake my head, even though I know he can tell it's a lie. "No … it's just …"

"What?" he prompts.

"I'm in your *home*," I say hollowly.

He grins. "You are."

"Why?"

He pauses, considering the question. The real question. Why did he allow me here? Into his private space? His gaze returns to meet mine, and he answers simply, "Because I thought, rather than a desk or the floor, you'd prefer to be fucked on something more comfortable."

My face reddens.

He chuckles. "Am I wrong?"

I smirk at him. "You're not wrong."

The amusement on his face grows, and he takes a sip of wine. "So, English major," he says. "What are you planning to do with that?"

I'm somewhat taken aback. Surprised at his question, surprised he cares enough to ask. And while I'm used to this same question asked with derision, the idea of an English degree being utterly useless, his isn't phrased that way. He's genuinely interested.

I smile, excited, as I always am, to talk about my future job. "I'm going to work in publishing," I tell him. "I already have a job lined up with a house here in Seattle."

Professor Henry raises his eyebrows. "Wow," he compliments. "That's incredible."

I nod. "I'm so excited. It's been my dream since I was a little kid. I can't wait to start."

"I'm sure you'll do great," he says.

I smile into my wine, suddenly embarrassed. I hope I'll do great. It's everything I ever wanted.

"What about you?" I change the focus of the conversation to him. "I saw on Kensington's website that you graduated from a school in LA. What made you come out here to Seattle?"

He seems surprised that I know this about him. That I looked him up. And while maybe I should feel embarrassed about it, I don't. It's public information. It's on Kensington's website.

He shrugs. "I was offered a job, I have family in the area. I also … needed to get away from LA."

There's something behind that last statement. Something that makes me think of the blonde in his Facebook photos. "Was it a bad situation?" I ask carefully, pressing for more.

He swirls the wine in his glass, staring down at it. "You could say that."

"I …" I stutter, suddenly feeling guilty about knowing more about him than I should. Maybe I should just come clean. "I know you were engaged once," I blurt out.

He looks up to meet my gaze, startled. "What?"

I grimace. "I looked you up on Facebook," I admit. "I'm sorry, that was probably weird. I just … wanted to know more about you. It was after we'd agreed on this … whatever we're doing—and I just wanted to know about you."

Suddenly, he laughs, surprising me. "You Facebook stalked me," he says evenly, and I feel myself flushing. He levels me with that intense look of his, amusement crinkling around his eyes. "Naughty girl."

The statement sends a wave of arousal through me. Is he going to use that as an excuse to do more of what he did to me yesterday? I can't say I mind the thought.

He chuckles again. "In the spirit of being honest, I did the same with you."

I widen my eyes in surprise, a laugh bubbling out of me. "You Facebook stalked me too?"

He nods, although unlike my admission, he seems to feel no shame. "Grew up here in Seattle, won a few poetry contests over the years, heading off to work at some prestigious publishing company. You're talented."

I blush, suddenly feeling even more on display. It's one thing to see me naked, it's another to see my past, my accomplishments, the things I'm most proud of. And *compliment* me on it. A warm feeling settles in my stomach.

"So what happened?" I throw the ball back in his court. "With ... *her*."

He pauses, and for a moment I worry I've pushed too far. But then he sighs, continuing to twirl the wine in his glass. "Things ended badly," he finally admits.

I'm silent, both because I hope he'll continue and because I don't know what to say.

"She cheated," he says evenly, his face devoid of expression. "So we ended things." He says it so nonchalantly, as if discussing the weather, but I can see the storm brewing behind his eyes. What she did devastated him. I can see it in his hardened jaw, the way his fingers tighten around the glass. But he's trying his best to hide it.

"Have you dated since?" I find myself asking. It feels both inappropriate and appropriate to ask. Inappropriate to ask of your professor. Appropriate to ask of someone who's done what Professor Henry has done to me.

He shakes his head. "Not in the traditional sense, no."

I frown. "What does that mean?"

He shoots me a soft smile. "As you know, I enjoy … a certain type of encounter."

I blush.

"Especially since …" But he trails off, shaking his head, not finishing the sentence. "A situation I can have absolute control over—consensually, of course."

Understanding washes over me. He hasn't dated. He's only done what he's done with me. Whatever that is. Suddenly insecure, I find myself asking, "Is there anyone else right now that you're …?" I can't quite find the right words.

A smile tugs at the corners of Professor Henry's lips. He shakes his head. "No Violet, just you."

The way he says it warms my belly.

"And never a student. Not until now." There's a reluctance to his tone, like he knows what we're doing is terribly, terribly wrong. Of course he knows. We both obviously know.

And yet we've walked into this willingly, and we're not stopping.

Taking the last sip of wine from my glass, I shoot Professor Henry a devilish grin. "So, I get to be fucked on something more comfortable than a desk tonight?" I tease him.

He laughs out loud, then leans toward me, taking my wine glass from my hands and setting it on the coffee table. "Only bad girls get fucked over desks, Violet. And you've been very, very good."

My breath catches in my throat as his hand slides slowly up my leg, under my skirt.

"Am I right?" he whispers in my ear, sending a shiver down my spine.

I don't know if he means about where I'd like to be fucked or whether I've been good, but I nod. Both. It's both.

His finger slides its way under my panties and glides along my entrance, making me gasp. "Good," he says. And with that, he stands, lifting me into his arms with him and striding across the room. I'm surprised he can carry me so easily as I'm not exactly petite, but he does so quite effortlessly.

He carries me through a doorway and into his bedroom, which is just as nicely decorated as the rest of the house, although sparser.

He sets me gently on the bed and reaches for the buttons of my shirt, slowly unbuttoning each one until he can pull my shirt off. He tosses it to the floor, then slides my skirt down my legs. I kick off my shoes.

He reaches behind me to unclasp my bra, stopping to run his hands across my breasts and down my body before pulling my panties off.

It's not until I'm fully naked on his bed that Professor Henry steps back to remove his own clothing. He pulls his gray shirt over his head, then steps out of his sweatpants, leaving nothing but dark blue boxers. I realize that this is the first time I've actually seen his body. He's always been fully clothed. While I've usually been completely bare and humiliated.

"Lie back," he says softly, and I do as he says.

He slowly climbs over top of me, stopping to kiss my belly and slowly drag his tongue up, up, up until it reaches one of my breasts, teasing my nipple.

I let out a high-pitched moan of contentment.

"You've been so good, Violet," he says. "Taking your punishment yesterday like a good girl."

I nod, my breathing increasing as he reaches up a hand to caress my other nipple.

"You took it so well," he says in between sucking my breast. "So submissive. So obedient."

I arch my back, my breasts begging for more from him.

"And I want to reward my obedient little student," he coos. "Make you cum so hard."

He pinches my nipple, eliciting a small gasp. He leans down so his lips brush my ear. "And no need to be quiet here," he purrs. "In fact, I intend to make you scream."

His words send my heart racing.

He climbs off of me, standing, and suddenly yanks my legs toward him until my ass is at the foot of the bed. He kneels between my knees, his gaze glued to mine. He fingers my entrance, slowly sliding a finger in and out of me, making me gasp.

"Such a good girl. So wet for me," he comments.

He removes his finger, and I arch my back, begging for more. He chuckles, looking up at me. "Good girls are submissive, Violet. Are you going to be a good girl?"

I nod.

"Manners," he reminds me.

"Yes, Professor," I say.

"Tell me to do whatever I want to you," he orders.

"Do whatever you want to do to me, Professor Henry," I breathe, relaxing back against the bed.

He smiles. Then he lowers his head, his tongue gliding along my entrance. I resist the urge to buck at the pleasure. It feels so unbearably good. His tongue makes slow, lazy circles around my clit, and I moan.

He reaches up a hand to pinch one of my nipples, and I cry out.

His tongue explores lower until it finds my entrance, slowly entering me. I moan, wanting more, more, more.

"Please, Professor," I whine.

He lifts his head, his fingers taking its place, drawing circles around my bud. "Please, what?" he asks.

"More," is all I can say, resisting the urge to writhe in pleasure. My body is on fire. His touch is somehow overwhelming and underwhelming at the same time. It's pure heaven and yet I need *more*.

"Tell me what you want me to do, Violet," he says. "You've been good. You can ask me."

I lift my head, meeting his gaze. His expression is calm, collected, aroused, while I know mine is desperate. "Fuck me," I say. "Please."

"Say it again," he orders.

"Please fuck me, Professor," I beg.

He stands, and I reel from his lack of touch. He pulls down his boxers, letting them fall to the floor, and I realize this is the first time I've seen Professor Henry fully naked. We're both fully naked in his room, on his bed. He pulls a condom from the drawer to his left, opening it and sliding it on.

"Sit up," he commands, and I do as he says. He pulls me from the bed so I'm standing, and then he takes a seat on the corner. He pulls me over to him and turns me around. It isn't until now that I realize there's a dressing mirror in the corner of the room. I see my naked reflection, Professor Henry sitting on the bed behind me.

He gently pulls me down onto his lap, and I feel his hardness. His hand against my stomach, he guides me backward until I feel his cock at my entrance. I sigh as he enters me, my pussy seeming to finally get used to his size. Even so, it's overwhelming in the best possible way.

"Good girl," he breathes in my ear, and if I could get wetter, I would. I melt into his body, my head leaning back against his shoulder.

He grips either side of my hips and starts rocking me back and forth, slowly at the first. I moan as his cock fills me even more than I thought possible, rubbing against the top of my pussy and creating a feeling I didn't know existed. All I can think of is this—nothing but Professor Henry's cock inside of me, filling me up, giving me an indescribable pleasure.

He starts rocking me faster, his own hips thrusting to meet the pace. I cry out and grip his arms, my nails digging into his skin. I catch a glimpse of myself in the mirror. My legs spread over his, his dick inside my pussy, my breasts jiggling as he rocks me back and forth.

"That feel good, Violet?" he asks, his own voice strained from pleasure.

"Yes, Professor," I cry.

"You like my cock inside you?"

"Yes, Professor." I'm nodding frantically.

"Keep moving," he orders. His hands leave my hips, and I work to keep up the momentum.

His hands reach up to cup my breasts, rolling my nipples between his fingers. My cries become louder, more desperate. He pinches them, and I shriek, arching my back and rocking faster.

One of his hands leaves my breast and migrates lower, finding my clit and rubbing slow circles that become faster. My cries are practically hysterical now. I can't control them. All I can think of is the pressure building inside me. The pleasure Professor Henry is somehow able to bring out of me. I want this to go on forever, and yet I feel that if I don't come *now,* I'll absolutely fall apart.

"*Professor,*" I sob, my head leaning back against his shoulder in absolute exhaustion.

"Yes, Violet?" he asks, and I never know how he can remain so calm. Doesn't he feel this same ecstasy? This inability to think past this pure pleasure?

"Can I come?" I beg. "Please, I need to come."

"Such a good girl for asking," he says, and his strokes along my clit become faster.

I see my face in the mirror, my mouth open in an inaudible gasp.

"Yes, sweetheart, I'm going to make you cum," he says into my ear. "And when you do, I want you to scream."

I nod, yelping with each rock of my hips.

"Is that a yes?"

"Yes, Professor," I say.

"Good girl."

He starts rocking faster, circling my clit faster, rubbing my nipple harder, and I feel the pressure building within me. My moans are louder, sometimes coming out in a cry I've never heard from myself. I'm practically sobbing, waiting for a release I desperately need.

"Oh *god,*" I scream, throwing my head back and climaxing like I've never done before. My legs spasm beneath me, and I feel my pussy clench and unclench in waves that seem to never end.

Professor Henry stands, lifting me with him, and lying me back on the bed. I notice he's still hard and that he must not have come yet. My chest rises and falls as I pant from my orgasm. Professor Henry, still standing, spreads my legs apart and enters me again. I'm still feeling the pulses from my orgasm as he starts pumping again, and I close my eyes at the soft pleasure of his cock filling me.

He thrusts harder and harder, my breasts jiggling with the impact, until he stills with a deep sigh and pulls from within me.

He stands, panting, looking down at me. I'm spent from the orgasm, still practically shaking.

"Are you going to be a good girl and come back here tomorrow?" he asks.

"Yes, Professor," I answer, looking up at him. I slowly sit up, still exhausted but aware enough to be slightly embarrassed by my nudity again. I reach for my underwear, damp from my wetness.

"Are you going to thank me for your reward?" he asks, putting on his own underwear as well.

Considering this was the best orgasm of my life, I smile and look him straight in the eyes. "Thank you for making me cum so hard I screamed, Professor Henry."

And I don't know if it was just a trick of the light, but I swear I see him blush just a little. And that blush triggers something within me. Something that starts on a high but then settles in the pit of my stomach. Oh no.

This situation—whatever we're doing—can only every stay the way it is. But there's a tiny, tiny

sensation growing within me. Some inscrutable
emotion I'm trying desperately to ignore.

Feelings. Real, actual feelings.

Fuck.

Chapter 13

Kayla and Matt are away again for the weekend, so I spend it mostly alone. I take the time to catch up on chores that need done—laundry, dishes, graduation prep, and homework assignments. All the while though, I can't stop thinking about Professor Henry. Only this time, it's different. Instead of just thinking of what he'd done to me, how he talked to me, how he made me feel … now I'm thinking about other things as well.

The way dimples appear on his cheeks when he smiles, the way he absentmindedly runs his fingers through his hair, the way he'd blushed when we'd last had sex.

Fuck. This can't be happening. It can't. Because I know what comes next.

It always happens like this. Always. I find a cute guy, we hook up, we keep hooking up, and eventually … I catch feelings. Usually small, but feelings nonetheless. And at this point, I've boiled it down to a science. When the feelings come, the men leave.

It's the way of the world. Nature, if you will. With me, at least. I don't know what it is. It must be something about me. Fuckable, but not lovable.

Jesus, that sounds terrible. I physically wince. I try not to spend much time dwelling on that conclusion I've come to, but sometimes I can't help it. And it hurts.

But I'm not in the mood for entertaining that thought today. Besides, my situation with Professor Henry is different. He's not anyone I ever *could* have dated. It's not like he's a normal guy I met off Tinder or at a bar. He's my *professor*. And our sexual relationship is literally transactional.

147

I'm shocked and frustrated with myself. I can't believe I could have let my guard down enough to develop … whatever it is I've developed for him.

Ugh.

I shove those thoughts from my mind, focusing on my homework assignment in front of me. It's one of my last essay assignments for one of my English classes, and while the work isn't difficult, there's a lot of it. I spent the rest of the afternoon typing away on my laptop, losing track of time.

I'm surprised when the door to the apartment opens and Kayla walks through. It's Sunday evening, so she and Matt must be back from their weekend getaway. I glance up and call out a greeting.

Kayla strides into the room, beaming—glowing. Immediately, I know something is different. I grin at her in confusion, about to ask what's going on, but she beats me to it.

"Matt proposed!" she declares, skipping up to me and presenting her hand, a large, shimmering diamond gleaming on her ring finger.

I stare down at it in shock. *Oh my god.* "Oh my god!" I exclaim.

"Right?" she squeals, plopping down on the couch beside me. "He proposed when we were out to dinner last night. He put it in a glass of champagne. Cliché, I know, but it was so cute."

I smile, still in shock. Kayla's engaged. She's engaged. I mean, I guess she'd mentioned the possibility the other day. But I didn't think it would happen so immediately.

"Kayla, that's amazing," I say, reaching for her hand to further inspect her ring. She shows it off proudly. "The ring is beautiful," I admire. "He did a good job."

"Didn't he?" she agrees.

"Wow," I say, unable to think of anything else. Part of me feels guilty. What's this strange emotion I'm feeling? Shouldn't I be overjoyed for Kayla? Shouldn't I be over the moon for her happiness? I *am* happy for her. I really am. There's just something that feels ... like I'm being left behind.

Like everyone else in the world has someone to love them.

And I don't. I never do.

I shake my head. *It's not time for a pity party, Violet. This is Kayla's moment.*

I reach across the couch to hug her. "I'm so happy for you, Kayla," I tell her. "I'm so excited."

"Thanks," she giggles. "The wedding won't be for at least a year out. We have to move and everything, after all, but I'm so excited to start our new lives together."

I nod along, smiling.

Kayla continues gushing about her weekend with Matt, how she'd suspected he was going to propose, but how she'd been surprised and emotional anyway.

After a few minutes, she tells me she's going to spend the night at his place, but wanted to stop by and share the news with me. After grabbing a few things, she leaves, her infectious joyous energy leaving with her.

I sit in the silence of the apartment with a whirlwind of emotions. Too many to count and too many to deal with.

And while this may not be the best way to cope, there's only one thing on my mind that I want to distract myself with.

I pull out my phone and shoot off a text.

Chapter 14

When Professor Henry opens the door, he's wearing those same sweatpants again and a blue t-shirt. He smiles when he sees me. "Come in," he says, stepping aside, and I walk into his home.

It's meticulously neat, just like the last time I was here. He levels me with one of his intense, amused stares, and suddenly, I'm embarrassed. It's the first time I've contacted him. The first time I've initiated any of our meetups. And suddenly I'm wondering if that's even okay. If that's part of our "deal."

He doesn't seem to mind though.

"Hey," he says with a warm smile, closing the door behind me. "I'm glad you texted. Want anything to drink?" he offers.

I shake my head. "I'm good, thanks."

"Water?" he presses.

I shrug. "Sure."

He leaves the living room and comes back a few moments later with a glass of water. He hands it to me, gesturing for us to sit on his couch.

"I'm assuming you aren't here for homework help," he says playfully, shooting me a dirty grin.

I take a drink of water, then set the glass down. "No," I say with a chuckle, and then, before I lose my nerve, I add, "I want you to fuck my brains out."

And it is what I want. Exactly what I want. For Professor Henry to fuck me so hard that I forget about everything. About my jealousy around Kayla and Matt, my sadness of feeling left behind, even my burgeoning feelings for him. I want it all gone.

Professor Henry's eyes widen in amused surprise. "Oh?" he asks.

I nod, leaning toward him, reaching for him.

"Hold on," he says with a chuckle, grasping my hand and returning it to my lap. "You seem …" He cocks his head. "Off. Is everything okay?"

I flush slightly. Ugh. Can he really read me that well? I shake my head. "I'm fine," I assure him. "Everything's fine."

He nods slowly, staring me down. "You seem like you're lying," he eventually says.

That forces a laugh from me. The bluntness of it all. "I'm not *lying*," I sputter.

He chuckles. "But you're not telling the truth."

After a long pause, I sigh. "Okay. I'm having a weird day, and I thought seeing you would … help."

"That's nice." He grins slightly. "What made the day weird?"

I stare at him for a heartbeat. Is he … asking about my day? Trying to get me to open up to him? Why would he want that? But as the seconds tick by, I feel compelled to answer. "My best friend just got engaged," I admit. "Which is a good thing," I'm quick to add. "It's just …" I trail off.

"Just what?" Professor Henry prompts gently.

I sigh. "It's just—I guess I just feel … left out? Left behind? Jealous? I don't even know."

He nods, taking it in, his eyes surprisingly understanding.

"I've always wanted to be in love. Always. And it just seems to happen to everyone else except … me." My declaration hangs in the stillness around us, and I feel myself blushing deeper. I hadn't intended on being that honest, that real. I hadn't intended to bare my soul like this. And yet, the words are already out and there's no taking them back.

After a few heartbeats, I look up into Professor Henry's eyes, expecting to see judgement or pity. But instead, I see neither. Just a compassionate understanding I wasn't expecting.

He reaches out to run a hand along my arm, down my forearm, to grasp my hand. It's the most intimate gesture we've ever exchanged, and it sends electricity coursing through me.

"Your lack of ... *love*, as you put it, is not a reflection on you," he states evenly. "Trust me."

He holds my gaze, seemingly staring into my soul. After a long moment, he reaches out to brush a strand of hair behind my ear, keeping his hand cupped behind my neck. And then, slowly, he brings his lips to mine.

He kisses me softly, delicately. He deepens the kiss, gently coaxing my mouth open with his tongue. I melt into him as he wraps his arms around me and pulls me against his chest. Gripping his t-shirt in my hands, I deepen the kiss, butterflies dancing in my stomach.

His hands roam my body, down the sides of my waist, my thighs, them up my stomach, to my breasts. He slides his hands under my shirt, finding my breasts and tugging on them. He pinches one of my nipples, eliciting a soft moan from me.

He continues caressing my nipples, hardening them into tight buds, and suddenly he grabs my shirt and bra and yanks them up over my chest, exposing me. He breaks our kiss to look down at me, taking me in.

I can feel myself flushing, getting hotter and hotter. Professor Henry starts thumbing each of my nipples while watching my face for a reaction. I open my mouth in pleasure, my eyes fluttering closed.

"Spread your legs, sweetheart," he commands.

I swallow. I hurry to do as he says, spreading my legs wide beneath my skirt. He slowly reaches up my skirt, then he slides a finger under my panties, pulling them aside right at my entrance. I feel the cool air rush against my hot flesh.

He slides a finger along my entrance, and I gasp.

He grins. "So wet for me," he comments. "Such a good girl."

Professor Henry slides three fingers into me at once, and I moan, throwing my head back at the sensation. He curls his fingers against my sweet spot, and I whimper. He flicks one of my nipples, then rolls it between his fingers.

"I love hearing you moan like that," he murmurs, leaning forward to kiss and nibble my neck, continuing to pump his fingers in and out of me. "Lie back." He pushes me back against the couch, positioning himself between my legs.

Leaning forward, he takes one of my breasts into his mouth, running his tongue over my nipple. I sigh in ecstasy, melting into the cushions below me. After a few moments, he moves and does the same to the other breast until my nipples are red and swollen. When he's done, he glances up at me with devilish grin.

Then he reaches down to pull his sweatpants down far enough to free his already hard cock. Pulling a condom out of his pocket, he slips it on. I feel him at my entrance, and then he pushes inside of me, his body pressed against mine.

A low moan escapes from my lips as his cock fills me. Even though I've taken him before, his size is still a shock, and it stretches and stings. He sighs deeply in my ear as he starts pumping faster.

His hand wanders across my body, over my breasts, lower and lower until he finds my clit. He starts with slow circles, which force moan after moan from my mouth.

"Oh, god," I whimper.

"Yeah, Violet?" he murmurs in my ear. "You like that?"

I nod. As he thumbs my aching bud, pumping relentlessly in and out of my pussy, the pleasure is more than I can bear. I cry out in ecstasy.

And then he picks up speed, fucking me like his life depends on it. Stars dance before my vision, the pressure of his dick, the swirling of his fingers around my clit, the closeness of our bodies all too much.

"Say my name," he demands.

"Professor Henry," I moan.

"No," he says, leaning back far enough to look my in the eye, our faces barely inches apart. "Alex. Say Alex."

I stare at him in shock for a moment but am quickly overcome by pleasure again as he rubs my clit faster. I gasp. "Alex," I whisper.

He pins me with his gaze, thrusting into my harder.

"*Alex*," I cry. I'm cresting higher and higher. I'm unable to stop my cries, and with one last thrust, I explode, collapsing in extasy beneath Professor Henry. He follows seconds after me, stilling inside of me, then relaxing.

We lay like that for a moment, completely intertwined on his couch, panting, before he slowly gets up. We fix our clothing in silence, and suddenly it dawns on me what just happened. He'd asked me to call him *Alex*.

Alex. His first name. A much more intimate name. A *real* name. Could that mean—

"I was about to make dinner before you came over," Professor Henry interrupts my thoughts. "Don't feel obligated by any means, but if you're hungry, you're free to stay." He smiles at me. It's still that same cool, confident smile, but I detect a hint of hope there too.

And before I can weigh the pros and cons, decide what this—any of this—actually means, I find myself agreeing. "Yes," I say. "I'll stay."

Chapter 15

I spend the next day wandering around in a haze, thinking—oddly enough—not about my sex with Professor Henry last night, but rather, dinner.

He'd made spaghetti while I'd leaned against the counter opposite him watching as he swirled the pasta sauce in a pot on the stove. I'd teased him about his lack of spices until forcefully taking over and insisting he add oregano and basil.

Then we sat at his small dining table with our plates of spaghetti and glasses of red wine and simply talked. I'd told him about my experiences at Kensington, about my new job and how excited I am to start it. He'd told me about LA, about the beaches, the school where he'd gotten his master's and PhD.

The whole thing had felt so strangely like a *date*.

A normal date.

So much so, that I'm worried my giddy, little mind might be tripping dangerously close to an edge I can never come back from. Because it couldn't have been a date. It couldn't have.

My phone buzzes in my pocket as I make my way to the parking lot after my last class of the day. When I pull it out, a hot flush creeps up my cheeks. It's Professor Henry. And he wants me to come over again tonight.

I reply immediately, telling him I'll be over later, then I unlock my car and hop inside. I put my key into the ignition and turn. The car rumbles a bit and then stops.

"Come on," I mutter, turning the key again. But to my frustration, the car is dead. "Damnit."

I toss my keys in my lap in frustration, leaning my head against the steering wheel.

I guess I didn't fully escape that hefty car bill after all.

I shoot off a quick text to Professor Henry, telling him tonight won't work—car trouble. Then I start googling the nearest towing and repair shop.

An incoming call flashes across my screen, halting my search. It's Professor Henry. I pause. We've never spoken on the phone before. He never calls me. I answer hesitantly.

"Hey," his voice says through the line. "Your car being difficult again?"

"Yeah," I say. "Sorry. I should probably deal with it tonight."

"You know, it might just need a new battery."

"That's what I was thinking too," I agree.

"The auto store near campus has cheap batteries."

I almost laugh. "I'm going to take it to a repair shop. I'm not about to attempt to replace my own car battery."

Professor Henry chuckles through the phone. "I'm still on campus. Are you in the south parking lot? Wait there for me."

Before I can protest, he hangs up. I stare down at my phone in disbelief while a slow smile creeps across my face. As much as I don't want to inconvenience him, I'm touched at how adamantly he seems to want to help.

A few minutes later, I see Professor Henry's car pull up beside mine, and he hops out, already rolling up the sleeves of his button up. "Hey." He shoots me a grin that melts my insides.

"Hi," I greet him, stepping out of my car to follow him around to the front of it. He lifts the hood, inspecting the battery, and then he strides back to his car. "I'll be back in ten minutes tops," he tells me, getting in and driving off.

I lean against my car, fiddling on my phone while I wait.

As predicted, he's back within ten minutes, pulling a brand-new car battery out of the passenger seat beside him. He pats it, holding it up for me to see as he strolls to my car's open hood.

Curious, I look over his shoulder while he works. It doesn't take him long. He takes out the old battery, puts the new one in, fiddles around with a few things, then instructs me to get back in the car and try to turn it on.

I do, and to my delight, the car sputters to life. "Hell, yeah!" I say, leaning out the door with a grin.

Smiling, Professor Henry snaps my hood closed, wiping his hands on his slacks. "Much easier than going to a repair shop," he says, coming around the side of the car. "And less expensive too."

The door is open, and I'm sitting in my seat with my legs dangling over the side, outward. He stands close to me, leaning against the door frame, staring down at me.

"Speaking of that," I say. "How much do I owe you for the battery?"

He shakes his head.

I stare at him for a moment, then frown. "Come on," I insist.

"Don't worry about it," he says simply.

"I—" I start, but Professor Henry reaches out a finger to press against my lips, silencing me. He leans forward, and I almost think he's going to kiss me, but we're on campus, so I know he won't—even though it's late in the day and the parking lot is virtually empty. "So," he says. "Still want to come over tonight? Or do you have final projects that need your attention?"

I smile up at him. "I could make tonight work. I've finished pretty much everything important." And it's true. I'd finished my last essays and senior projects for

167

all my classes. It's crazy to think that graduation is pretty much the only thing left.

He raises an eyebrow. "So efficient," he praises. "A little genius."

I roll my eyes. "Yeah a genius who can't pass a basic biology class without sleeping with her professor." I mean it as a joke, but it comes out a bit more raw than I'd expected. A bit harsh.

Professor Henry's expression falters, and I see something in his eyes I haven't before. Is that … guilt?

"I hope you don't think that because you weren't doing well in my class, that—that you aren't intelligent," he says softly.

I give him a pointed look. "Who fails *basic* biology?" I shoot back with a chuckle, but it's forced.

Professor Henry frowns, staring down at me in deep thought. I look at him questioningly. "What?"

He opens his mouth as if to reply, but pauses, unable to find the words. "I …" he finally mutters, ducking his head. "I should tell you something."

Taken aback, I wait. What could he possibly have to tell me?

He looks back up, meeting my gaze, and in his eyes is an expression I've never seen before. Guilt, sorrow, pleading for … forgiveness? Why would he need my forgiveness?

"You weren't really failing my class," he says, almost in a whisper.

The words don't hit me right away. At first, they're just words. Meaningless sounds that have no effect. But slowly, they sink in. I stare up at him, the color slowly draining from my face.

"What?" is all I can think to utter.

Looking pained, he continues. "You weren't failing. You were doing fine. I …" He trails off, grimacing. "I wanted an excuse to speak with you more, to …" He shakes his head. "I was never going to keep your grade that way, regardless of what happened between us. I swear."

I suddenly feel as if the breath has all been knocked out of me. "You lied?" I say.

He doesn't respond, simply staring at me with eyes that beg for forgiveness. Forgiveness I'm not sure I can give.

"You lied so that I would sleep with you."

He looks as if I've physically hit him, but he doesn't defend himself. How can he? "It's inexcusable," he says quietly. "I know."

"Do you?" I snap, standing, pushing him a few steps back. "Oh my god." I brush past him, suddenly needing air, needing space. A few steps away, I twirl back around. "You made me think I was a failure. You manipulated me. And after yesterday, after this," I gesture to my car, "I was starting to think—" I stop myself suddenly. "It doesn't matter what I thought," I mutter.

"It matters," he insists. "What were you starting to think?" His question is quiet, laced with hope. But I can't spend the time to decipher what that means—all I can see is his deception.

A sudden lump forms in my throat, and I look away, furious at the idea of him seeing me cry.

"I'm so sorry, Violet," he says, and I hear him take a step toward me. I hold up my hand, and he stops. "I never meant for …" He never finishes his sentence. Because there's nothing he can say that will make this better. And I think he knows that.

Averting his gaze, I brush past him once again, getting into my car. Without a word, I slam the door shut and turn on the ignition. Professor Henry stoically moves aside as I pull out of my parking space and exit the parking lot.

It isn't until I'm out on the road leaving campus that I let myself cry.

Chapter 16

With graduation looming, I don't have time to dwell on Professor Henry. Which is good, because it I wasn't buried up to my shoulders in last minute assignments and graduation preparation, I know I'd be crying myself to sleep every night and moping around like my life was over.

I spend Professor Henry's classes barely listening, barely paying attention, barely putting in any effort. And the second class is done, I'm always the first out the door. I notice him trying to make eye contact with me, trying to casually stop me on my beeline to the door, but I always ignore him.

He tried calling the first few days after I left him standing alone in the campus parking lot. But I denied all his calls, knowing that hearing his voice would only make the hurt worse. Not only did he do the most unethical thing I can think of, but he lied to me about my abilities, made me think I was a failure when I wasn't. After a few days, the calls stopped coming anyway.

As the days turned into one week, and then two, the anger settled as well. But it was replaced by something much worse: hurt.

A deep, agonizing hurt. A hurt that touched a nerve deep inside me that I'd forgotten was there. A nerve I'd been trying to protect.

Because just like every other guy I've been with, all Professor Henry wanted was to sleep with me. And the second I started developing feelings, it went up in flames. I suppose I should have seen this coming. This was our arrangement, after all. I hadn't expected to *feel* anything for him, and yet … I did.

Which is why his betrayal stings so much more.

And it makes me wonder, deep down inside, whether I'm truly worthy of being loved at all. Cared for in the way that relationships make you feel cared for. Because, despite how badly I want it, no one ever seems to want a relationship with me.

A lump forms in my throat, and I immediately tamp down the feelings. Not now. This is not the time.

Kayla sits across from me on the floor in our apartment, an array of glitter, sparkly letters, and flowers spread out on the floor between us. We have glue guns and our graduation hats next to us, ready to decorate to our hearts' content.

"What color scheme are you going for?" she asks me, pulling me from my thoughts.

I cock my head. "I was thinking blue."

She nods. "It'll match your eyes. I'm going with yellow," she declares.

We start gluing on glitter and flowers, the TV playing in the background. "I'm going to miss you," I say suddenly.

She looks, up shooting me a sad smile. "I'm going to miss you too," she says. "But we'll visit each other. We'll talk on the phone. And we have exciting futures ahead of us," she reminds me. "I'm excited for my new program. And you have an incredible job lined up—an incredible career."

I smile. She's right. We do have things to look forward to. And my job starts in barely a week. The beginning of my new life. The life I've dreamed of since I was a kid.

Chapter 17

"I now present the newest graduates of Kensington University!" the announcer declares, and the audience roars with applause and cheers. I, along with the hundreds of students around me, toss my hat into the air.

Kayla laughs in glee beside me as we try desperately to catch our correct hats, diving into each other and giggling. Music plays, and students begin filing out of the auditorium. Kayla leans over to give me a hug.

"We did it!" she exclaims.

"We did it," I echo with a grin. "Look at us with our bachelor's degrees."

We file out of the auditorium, scanning the crowd for our families. I find mine—my parents and older brother—and quickly go over to greet them. They give me hugs and congratulations, and after a few moments of pictures and mingling, we head off to dinner, waving goodbye to Kayla and her family.

The rest of the night is spent celebrating, first with dinner with my family, and then with late-night drinks with Kayla, Matt, and a few other friends. We don't make it back to our apartment until the wee hours of the morning, and when we do, I immediately collapse into bed, thrilled with the day of celebration and relieved and accomplished to finally have graduated.

■■■ ı

The next morning, I wake up with a surprising lack of hangover despite how many drinks we'd had the night before. It must have been the water I'd insisted on chugging before going to bed. A Saturday, Kayla and I spend the morning hours lounging around the living room, watching reality TV and snacking.

A knock at the door around midday surprises both of us, and I get up to investigate. Opening the front door, I see a delivery woman standing on the other side, a large bouquet of flowers in her hand. "For Violet Sloan," she says.

"That's me," I say, numbly taking the bouquet. Who would have sent flowers? If they were from my family, they would have simply given them to me yesterday.

The woman shoots me a smile and then leaves, so I close the door.

"Ooooh, graduation flowers," Kayla says, ogling them from the couch. "Who are they from?"

179

"I'm not sure," I mutter, taking them to the kitchen and setting them on the counter. I reach for the tiny envelope pinned to one of the roses, opening it to find a note. *Congratulations*, it reads. It's signed with a simple *H*.

My stomach summersaults. Professor Henry. It has to be. There's no one else—especially who would sign the note *H*—who would send me flowers. I think back to yesterday. I know he'd been at the graduation. As a professor, he has to be. But I hadn't seen him. In fact, I'd been determined not to. I'd avoided glancing at the science professors' section entirely. But I just knew that his eyes were on me as I walked across the stage to receive my diploma. As much as I'd tried not to think about him, I couldn't help it.

A pang of longing stirs inside of me. I miss him. I really do. The realization is surprising and upsetting at the same time.

"Who are they from?" Kayla asks again.

I shake my head, leaving the flowers on the counter and returning to the couch. "No one important," I say.

But I should know that answer would only spark more curiosity, because Kayla's eyes widen, and she presses further, "Who?"

I sigh, unwilling to tell her the entire truth. "Just … some guy I was seeing very briefly."

"You were seeing someone?" Kayla asks, shocked.

"Yeah, but things … didn't end very well."

"Oh." She glances between me and the flowers on the kitchen counter. "He sent you flowers, though," she says softly, noticing my dour demeanor. "Does that mean things might not be over? If that's what you want, of course."

I shrug. "I think it's just an apology. He messed up. Big time."

She nods, pausing for a moment. "Is it something you want to forgive?"

I look at her. *Is* it something I want to forgive? Is it something I *could* forgive? "I don't know," I finally say.

Kayla chuckles. "Well, that's not a no."

I smile, glancing sideways at the flowers.

"You know, I gave Matt a second chance once."

I look back at her, surprised. This is the first I'm hearing of any turmoil in their relationship.

"It was early on. It was over something that felt big at the time, something that hurt me deeply. And I was prepared to walk away, I really was. But I changed my mind and decided to give him a second chance. And I'm glad I did," she says, throwing her hands up in the air. "If your heart is telling you not to hear this guy out, then definitely don't," she adds. "But sometimes people mess up and just need a chance to prove themselves."

Chapter 18

It's late, the streetlamps shining brightly down on the darkened street and the air hushed with nighttime as I stand outside Professor Henry's house and knock on his door.

He opens it, a shocked expression settling over his face when he sees me. "Violet," he says quietly, then, more quickly, "Come in."

He steps aside, and I enter his house. The TV is on, and he quickly reaches for the remote on the couch to turn it off, sending the room into silence. He looks at me uncertainly.

"Do you want to sit down?" he asks.

I nod, walking to the couch and taking a seat. The couch we'd had sex on not too long ago. The thought sends a pang of sadness through me. Seeing him at all sets my nerves on fire. Because despite all that he did, despite the logical part of my brain telling me I should leave, all I can think about is how desperately I miss him. How I want to talk over dinner, tease each other over stupid things, and feel his hands all over me.

"I got your flowers," I say, breaking the silence.

"Congratulations on graduating," he replies. "It's an important accomplishment. And suma cum laude," he adds, smiling, a sparkle in his eye. It's announced when you walk across the stage and receive your diploma—so it does mean he was watching me, listening. "Impressive."

I bite my lip, looking down. "I worked hard," I say simply.

The teasing slowly leaves his face, and he's suddenly serious. "You did," he states emphatically. "And you deserved it. I ..." He pauses for a moment, and I look up to watch his face. "I want to apologize again. What I did—it undermined everything you worked for, undermined who you are as a student." He looks me in the eyes, and for a moment I think he's about to reach out, but he doesn't. "You're *smart*, Violet," he tells me. "And that shit I pulled—it made you doubt that. And for that, I'll forever be sorry."

His apology settles in my chest, and I simply stare at him, unsure what to say.

He takes a deep breath. "After what happened with my ex—her cheating on me—my trust was destroyed. I only enter situations where I'm in complete control, in every way possible. It's the only way I can ..." He stops, running a hand through his hair. "It's not an excuse, it's not a justification, but it is a reason. And I ... I need to stop."

Suddenly, Professor Henry has gone from the reserved, stone-faced, confident man I've always seen to someone vulnerable, exposed. He rests his hand on his knee, his fist clenched.

"And more importantly, you didn't deserve that. You *don't* deserve that," he goes on. He meets my gaze, and the intensity is back, pinning me to the spot. "I felt real things with you, Violet. For the first time in years. And I understand if you never want to see me again after this, I truly do. But I just needed you to know. And to thank you."

Silence surrounds us for a few heartbeats as I take in his words. What happened with his ex, how hurt he must have been, his reasons for why he started our situation, and then … that last part. That last part keeps getting caught in my head, dissected into tiny, tiny pieces. Because did I hear him right? Did he say he *felt* things? In the same way that I did too?

I'm trying to formulate some response, something to say, but Professor Henry gets up before I can respond. He walks across the room, retrieving something from the bookshelf against the wall and then returning to the couch. "I was going to send you this along with the flowers," he says, staring down at the slim book in his hands. "But I didn't want it—I didn't want it to feel manipulative. To influence your feelings about me or any decisions you made." He frowns, as if regretting his choice to grab it just now. "But I want you to have it." He hands it to me.

I take it from him gently, glancing down at it. It's a poetry book. Contemporary poetry. The kind I write— the kind I'd won contests writing in high school and early college. I guess he knew I wrote poetry, but I never thought he'd care to look into it. I skim through the pages, glancing at titles.

Then, on the title page, I see a handwritten note.

> *I want you to know you're worthy of*
> *love. More love than even these*
> *poems could hold.*

> *– Alex*

My breath catches in my throat. I frown, fighting back the emotions bubbling up inside of me. Happiness, joy, confusion, tears. I look up to meet

Professor Henry's—Alex's—gaze, and he stares back at me with an expression mixed with trepidation, pleading, and sadness.

"I understand if you never want to see me again, Violet," he repeats.

"I don't think I could do that," I find myself saying before I even have time to consider the implications. "I want … you," I say quietly.

A smile washes over Alex's face, and he reaches for me, grabbing my wrist and then trailing his hand up my arm. "I want *you*, Violet," he murmurs. "And not just for sex. For everything."

I laugh, both of giddy relief and from the absurdity. "Everything?" I repeat.

He grins. "Everything. Dinner, dates, walks on the beach, helping you with that stupid car." He chuckles.

"You're definitely going to have to keep helping me with that car," I laugh.

He smiles, leaning in closer, brushing his lips against my ear. "And fucking you in ways I know you like being fucked."

Warmth pools in my lower belly, and I sigh quietly. "I'm not your student anymore," I say, biting my lip. "Does that make it a little less hot?" I tease.

He leans back and smirks. "I think you're always going to be teacher's pet."

With that, he hooks an arm under my knees and another around my back, and swoops me into the air. I laugh in surprise, and he carries me across the living room, down the hall, and into his bedroom.

He gently lays me down on the bed, trailing kisses down my neck, my collarbone, and my chest. He deftly unbuttons the front of my dress as he goes, kissing the tops of my breasts, down my stomach, my belly button, to my navel. When he's done with all the buttons, I sit up, and he helps me shrug out of the dress.

He reaches around to unclasp my bra, tossing it to the side, then lowers his mouth to my breast. He runs his tongue in circles around my nipple, and I sigh deeply, relaxing into the mattress. Trailing his tongue across my chest to my other breast, he does the same there until I'm a moaning, whimpering mess.

Continuing his perusal, he kisses his way down my stomach and down my thighs, then gently pulls my panties down my legs, discarding them. A hand on each knee, he spreads my legs before him, taking in the sight of me. I lie there, panting, on full display, waiting for whatever he has next in store.

Shooting me a wicked grin, he lowers his mouth to my center, running his tongue along my slit. I moan, bucking my hips, but he places a hand over my lower belly, holding me down. He runs his tongue along my bud, eliciting deeper and deeper moans the faster he goes.

I grab fistfuls of the blanket beneath me, writhing in pleasure as he continues. The pressure builds and builds, and finally, with a cry, my orgasm hits me. Alex leans back then climbs over me as I lie there panting from my orgasm.

He presses his body against mine, his lips against my ear. "You like being teacher's pet?" he murmurs.

I smile and nod. "Yes, Alex," I say.

He pulls back to look me in the eye, the most genuine smile I've seen from him plastered on his face.

He gets off the bed momentarily, shedding his t-shirt, sweatpants, and boxers, pulling a condom from the nightstand, and putting it on. He climbs back across the bed, nestling himself between my thighs and pressing his body against me. He presses his lips to mine, kissing me long and deep until I'm breathless. Our lips still locked together, I feel him at my entrance, and then he slowly pushes inside.

I break our kiss to gasp in pleasure, and he sighs against my parted lips. "That's my good girl," he breathes as he starts thrusting.

My nails dig into the flesh of his back, gripping him for dear life as his cock hits my g-spot over and over again, filling me deeper and deeper. Alex snakes a hand between us to find my clit, rubbing it as he continues to pump in and out of me.

I cry out, gripping him tighter.

"That's it, sweetheart," he murmurs, picking up speed.

"Oh god," I cry. "*Alex.*"

"Yeah, baby?"

"Alex!" I cry, climaxing for the second time, my legs shaking violently. Seconds later, he finishes too, stilling inside of me, and then relaxing against my body. We lie there for a moment, catching our breath.

Alex presses a kiss to my cheek, and I smile. He runs a finger along the side of my face, gently brushing a strand of hair behind my ear. "My favorite student," he says teasingly and lovingly at the same time.

I laugh, throwing my head back. I meet his gaze, giggling as I reply, "My favorite professor."

Penelope Ryan

Penelope Ryan writes steaming-hot contemporary romance with sweet yet filthy male leads. Whether they include a hot billionaire, a sexy professor, or just a gorgeous hunk who's great at dirty talk, Ryan's books are as hot as they come.

Other novels by Penelope Ryan:

The Billionaire's Assistant

The Billionaire's Obsession

The Billionaire's Wife

My Best Friend's Billionaire Brother

Tempting the Billionaire

Losing It

The Arrangement

Want a free Penelope Ryan novel? Head over to

penelope-ryan-books.com and click "Free Book!" at the top to claim your copy!

Made in the USA
Las Vegas, NV
02 January 2025